THE LOST HEIR OF ISLA

REALMS OF DESTINY
BOOK ONE

LYSSA LUND

For my Dad and Mom, Neil, and Jeanne.

I can't imagine there being two more supportive and giving parents on this earth. I am so blessed to call you mine.

WORLDS COLLIDE

erron Matthews had been my best friend since I was a toddler.

His once rambunctious, playful behavior was what drew me to him. Things had certainly changed since then—mostly because of the hostile takeover of our home realm and the slaughter of our prominent, powerful parents, which would understandably ruin anyone's normal, happy-go-lucky outlook.

"Dammit, Ophelia, stay down," he muttered under his breath.

The pistol in his hands glinted under the flickering light of the parking garage's third floor. I eyed it carefully, hating how he carried it around all the time. Tonight though, it came in handy. We had been having another night in, the same as we did every night.

Terron called it *flying under the radar*, but seeing as we had escaped many realms away from our home world and settled down in a rural town outside Cheyenne, Wyoming, I'd say we couldn't be more under the radar if we tried.

"Why can't we sneak down those stairs?" I breathed, panting with each word.

The run from our apartment was hard enough after being woken up past midnight. Now we had to figure out how to get to the bottom level of the parking garage without being shot or captured. I eyed the stairs not far away, daring to lean forward and bolt toward them, but Terron pinned me down, preventing any movement.

"Ophelia, please. Let me handle this."

We both flinched as a bullet entered one side of the car where we hid and exited the other side, mere inches from us. We looked at each other for a moment, and then we were running. Terron kept a firm grip on my upper arm, having to slow down to accommodate my speed.

He was over six feet tall, with muscles he had built throughout our time in the mortal realm. He hadn't had a lot of time to do much else, and since we were trying to fit into this world without being discovered, he thought it would be a good opportunity to look like a muscle man who deemed it necessary to run like a freshly born deer.

He uttered something under his breath before throwing me into the stairwell. I caught myself on the first few steps, clinging to the handrail to stay upright. A hail of gunfire was set loose on us both. Terron leaned back into the parking garage once, then twice, firing back at the culprits who broke into our apartment in the middle of the night.

These men weren't mortal burglars.

They were hunters from our home realm, Isla.

I eyed the bottom of the stairs, seeing movement through the handrails. I panicked, reaching for Terron to warn him, but when he took his eyes off the parking garage in front of us, a stray bullet flew upward, grazing his hip. He held back a scream, instead pointing his pistol through the railing and firing back.

"Agh!" a voice hollered from downstairs.

"Can't go down there," Terron groaned, one palm pressed into his wound, the other trying to fight off the gunfire from the third-story level where we were trapped. "Can't go that way either," he added, looking straight ahead.

"Terron, we have to go," I pleaded, my heart racing so loud I mistook the gunfire from the lower level as my own rapid thudding pulse. I watched a set of hunters ascend the stairs, trapping us. "Ter—"

He hooked an arm around my hips, pulling me out of the gunfire in the parking garage and hiking me over the third-floor railing. My hands went cold and clammy, watching him dive headfirst over the railing, taking me with him.

Before I could scream, the air was snatched from my lungs, landing hard on Terron as we hit the grassy knoll below. I rolled off of his chest, and my ankle twisted from the landing. I reached for him, his eyes blinking slowly. Landing on his back from such a height was not exactly ideal, let alone my using his chest to break my fall.

"Please, Terron, get up—they're coming," I begged, helping him crawl to a stand, his eyes glancing upwards toward the tall railing. I did the same, discovering hunters in all-black clothes leaning over the barrier we jumped over, their guns already leveled at us from up there. "Oh no—"

There was a shot.

Terron threw me over his shoulder and ran with a limp. His quick thinking and strategic parking spot may have saved our lives again. I finally heard the car purr to life and felt the engine under us. Terron kept me in his lap, sitting crookedly against his chest while he kicked the car into drive and sped away into the night.

I didn't bother asking if we were being followed. The Wyoming night sky was in full bloom with thousands of stars overhead, each one whizzing by as Terron slammed down on the gas pedal. The air in my lungs finally returned, and I inhaled, my eyelids dropping shut once, then twice before I realized I was hurt.

"Ouch," I mumbled, trying to scoot off Terron's lap and feeling a sharp pressure in my back. I reached around and discovered a small metal rod indented into the back of my shoulder. My breath caught, and my fingers came back bloody when I settled into the passenger seat. "Was I—was I shot?"

Terron looked over, checking the highway shoulder before we pulled over, his hands leaving the wheel as he reached for my shoulder. I pulled my long, white hair aside, the ends stained red from my blood. I could practically taste it. Terron mumbled something to himself, his fingers brushing the wound before the long, silver cap was yanked from my shoulder blade.

I released a scream, seeing spots. My head fell back off the side of the seat, watching him examine the capsule in his crimson-stained fingers.

"It's not a bullet, Ophelia," he said, holding it to the light of the car's dashboard. "It's a tranquilizer. They weren't trying to kill you; they were going to—" My heart dropped, hearing the meaning behind the words he didn't say out loud. He tossed the capsule in the back seat, reaching for me.

I curled into my his arms, feeling the drowsy effects start to haunt my system.

"Why would they try to sedate me?"

Terron held me tighter, his hand pressing firmly on the back of my head, allowing me to weep gently into his neck. "I don't know for sure, but we always knew this could happen. I wasn't anticipating it until *after* your nineteenth birthday."

"Is it Jull?" His name was like fire on my tongue.

He pressed his fingers against the mark on my shoulder, only recoiling when I hissed. He didn't answer my question,

4

which should be answer enough. It was always a possibility that the monster who murdered our parents and forced us to flee our home realm would be crawling back to finish off the next generation, but I was hopeful he wouldn't find us.

My eyes begin to close. The world slowed down around me, as though Earth decided it was done spinning for the night.

"I don't want to go back," I breathed, clinging to Terron so tight I refused to let him go until I passed out of consciousness for good. Judging by my migraine, I'd say I didn't have long to wait. "Please, don't let them take me, Terron."

"I won't, don't worry," he hummed, squeezing me once. "I promised your father I'd protect you. If they think ambushing us is going to work, it won't. I will keep you safe, trust me."

I felt my arms go limp, then the rest of my body followed shortly after. Terron settled me back into my seat, and my world went dark.

That's when I see Jull.

He's a thin, beanpole of a man. He was always tall, but in my younger years, I would stare up at the man my father was constantly at odds with. He would look down at me as though I was a little bug in his path, begging to be squished under his polished leather boots.

My father was a powerful, influential man with our world at his fingertips. Everything changed when Jull attacked the advisors. They were killed in the capitol, the place they spent most of their lives, protecting the realms and keeping peace in Isla. It was another work day, and I was playing in the halls with my best buddy, Terron.

We were chasing one another through the halls, running so fast it was like we were flying. I had never laughed so hard in my life, and I hadn't laughed like that since. I was speeding down the hall toward the conference room where my dad spent most of his days. That's when I slammed into a pair of tall, lanky legs.

Terron came to my side and tucked me behind his back. He was seventeen at the time, and I was twelve. I couldn't imagine not being intimidated by Jull, but Terron feared very little. He apologized on my behalf, mentioning that both of our fathers were busy at work, and I realized now it was to deter Jull from interrupting them.

My father was the Head Advisor. Sort of like the king of a palace, while Terron's dad was his second in command as the advisor to war relations. Terron is a strategist like his father, and when Jull looked past him, shooting me a scathing glare, Terron stepped in the way and gave it right back to the lanky blowhard.

"Aww, what a gentleman," Jull hummed, his voice like the hissing growl of a snake. "Look at you, protecting the unfit offspring of Head Advisor Marshal."

His words stung. At the time, I was already aware of my unfortunate birth. Head advisors are supposed to be replaced by their bloodline, each one acquiring an enchanted gift on their nineteenth birthday, making them capable of assuming the position held by their father.

There was one small problem with me.

My father had a girl.

My mother passed before they could try for a son, but the damage was done. I was marked as unfit offspring to be an advisor. I was the mistake running the halls, the miscreant girl who usually kept her head down, all except for this day.

"I suggest you keep up the good work," Jull hummed, eyeing the conference room doorway. "She's going to need all the help she can get."

When Jull left us alone, I thought we were safe to resume playing.

The gunfire that followed had other plans.

PARADOX

"*R*elax, shh, it's okay," Terron breathed.

I jolted upright in an unfamiliar bed, my forehead and neck covered in a thick sheen of sweat. My hands were shivering like I was cold, contradicting the heat rising through my throat. I reached for the spot on my shoulder where I recalled the tranquilizer protruding from.

Thankfully, he was resourceful enough to cover the wound. My ankle was also wrapped tightly in a thick gauze tape. I was still panting, recalling the nightmare I wished wasn't weaved in truth.

I shot into Terron's arms, holding him tight as the relapse of misery and fear overcame me, and the memories flooded my system immediately. I glanced over his broad shoulder, noticing the quaint hotel room we were staying in right now, the walls a cream color with generic, abstract art hammered into the drywall.

"Hotel?" I asked under my breath.

Terron pulled back, tucking my blood-stained hair

behind my ear. "Yeah, for now, Ophelia. It won't be long before we find another home, though. Don't worry."

My stomach knotted. "Another home? So I guess we can't go back to Cheyenne?"

He looked dejected, his icy eyes scanning the go-bag of clothes we had stowed away in the car in case we ever had to make a quick run for it. It was only a few items of clothing and a couple of wads of cash, but it was all we had now.

"Look at this as a positive, O. It's going to all work out—it always does."

"What if they find us again?"

"We will just keep moving," he said reassuringly, although it was hard to tell if he was trying to convince me or himself. "I have kept us safe so far. I can continue to do so, even if we have to start over. Everything will be fine, I promise."

"They came from our realm," I breathed, my hands trembling in my lap. "They found us on one of the easiest planets for us to blend in on, and they still tracked us down, Terron. Do you think moving states is going to keep them at bay? Should we go back to Topree?"

I tried to flush out the memories of our short stint in the horrid realm. We were so young when the takeover occurred that we knew we couldn't make lives on Earth yet without being questioned as to why a pair of adolescent teenagers were running around solo. There were no laws in Topree, and free-roaming youths were the norm there, with a hint of danger added in as well.

Terron winced at the mere mention of the underworld market realm. It was nothing but chaos and trouble in Topree, where the landscape was terrifyingly deserted with sand and swindlers. We wouldn't last there for long, but with Jull sending his men to Earth, we might not be safe here. It might be the only option.

I fought back the tears swelling in my eyes, knowing for

certain they traveled worlds away to find us here and wouldn't give up at the first sign of resistance. They would come back for me, and Terron knew that, too.

"They were trying to kill us," I wept.

"No, they were trying to kill me," he said, his focus elsewhere as though his mind was wandering other worlds in his head. "They were trying to keep you alive. They wanted to take you with them, but I can't understand why."

"Jull hates me," I said. "He would want to kill me himself, I'm sure of it."

"He assumed the advisor titles years ago when he stormed the capital of Isla. This has to do with your birthday, Ophelia. Otherwise, it wouldn't matter if we lived or died. He must be curious about your gift."

I felt my heart hollow out with his words. When Terron turned nineteen in this realm, he was given the same gift as his father. He was a strategist by blood, so it was only fitting when he was awarded enhanced gifts of tracking and surviving. He was a master at strategy regarding life longevity.

I was thankful for his gift today—and especially yesterday.

"Let's take a break here for a day. We can leave when we're well rested and hopefully find a new home before your birthday tomorrow." Terron stood, stretching his sore muscles, his shirtless physique tainted with bruises lining his back and a dressed wound on his side. I looked away from his wounds, the sight making me ill. "Stay in the room. I'm going to go grab us something from the corner store. All right?"

"Yeah, okay," I agreed.

I retreated to the shower when he left, finally getting to wash the dried, maroon blood out of my long, ivory hair. I kept on my necklace, an heirloom of my mother's. It was a moonstone opal, rare in our realm but filled with so much beauty, so much strength, it was practically impenetrable.

Once upon a time, I thought it was symbolic of me.

Now I thought it was a pretty stone, given to a pretty face who wasn't worth the trouble it would take to break the trinket in half. At least, I thought that was the case. Jull had something planned, and whatever it was, it had to do with me.

Wrapped in a hotel towel, I planned to dig through the go-bag and find an outfit to slip into, but when I entered the bedroom, I stopped cold in my tracks.

A man paced the window of the bedroom, his hands meticulously folded behind his back, his eyes glaring out into the parking lot through a gap in the blinds. I didn't know whether to run or scream—both options rather futile if he indeed worked for Jull.

He turned slightly, not facing me all the way but enough for me to catch a glimpse of his emerald eyes. He was meticulously dressed and gave off an air of superiority, an obvious sign he had come from Isla. He certainly stuck out in this realm with his cold, porcelain exterior and brightly lit irises.

"Ophelia. It's been a long time."

I remained frozen in place, my eyes tracing his long, black trench coat and wondering how many deadly weapons he had hidden under the lengthy cover. I didn't have to consider my options for long, the door to the room flew open, and my hands clenched my towel tighter, thankful when I saw Terron barging in.

He tossed the groceries aside, his hands wielding two chrome pistols instead. "Who the heck is this?"

I stepped back, ready to dive into the bathroom at the first sign of gunfire. "I don't know, Terron. He was in here when I got out of the shower."

"Terron Matthews. What a surprise seeing you in this

realm," the stranger hummed. He finally turned around completely, his high cheekbones and perfect jawline something from an old artist's best dream. He looked through both of us, his thoughts written clearly on his face. "I should have anticipated you two would have stuck together through the years. You both were always so close growing up. Too close for comfort at times."

I scrunched my nose at the insinuation. Terron was like my older brother, always had been, which made me wonder how this stranger knew us both and our history from so long ago, considering I couldn't seem to figure out who he was and how he knew us so well. Either way, the thought of Terron and I being an item wasn't further from the truth. He was my protector, my guard dog, and right now, he acted like he could chew into this asshole without remorse.

Terron lowered the guns after a moment of consideration, his head cocked in confusion. "Sig Hughes? It can't be you."

The man bowed obnoxiously. "In the flesh."

"Hughes," I mumbled, my mind working overtime to piece together the puzzle before me. "Hughes was an advisor in Isla. The—the—"

"Advisor of foreign realms, of course," Sig replied. He smiled wide, a friendly grin making his identity more recognizable than before.

Sig Hughes was a childhood bully by nature and more often than not, I was his easiest victim. Everyone was already considering me Isla's most worthless offspring of an advisor, and when word spread through school some advisors considered me better off dead than alive to assume control. Sig took it upon himself to make my childhood days horrible.

"I should apologize for my past behavior," Sig mumbled,

obviously working through the same past conflicts I was right now.

"Forget it. I'm so happy to see another one of us is alive."

"Which brings me to my next question," Terron said while forcing me behind his towering presence. *"How* are you alive?"

Sig didn't seem as offended as I would be if asked that question. If Terron wanted to know if Sig was some kind of inside worker for Jull and his goons, he could have come out and asked it rather than making it an uneasy moment with his accusatory tone.

Our old acquaintance smiled candidly. "I have hopped back and forth from Topree to Earth in my time since the overthrow. I typically try to avoid this realm for long stretches of time, but when I overheard Jull was sending some of his combatants out to track down a particularly gifted girl, I had a feeling it involved you. I wanted to see what all the fuss was about."

My brow furrowed. "I don't have my gift yet."

Terron shot me a narrow, commanding gaze. I knew the look well in our time together and instantly shut my mouth. He examined Sig, his eyes pacing the young bully we used to fight back and forth with on the playground growing up.

"Did they mention why else he may have wanted her?" Terron asked.

Sig stalled for a second, glancing out the windows and watching the parking lot like he had been doing when I first discovered him in the room. "She's the daughter of Head Advisor Marshal. I can only assume the interest involves her lineage. From what I hear, things in Isla have been going downhill since the hostile takeover. Jull is grasping for solutions. This could be part of his scheme."

I shivered, soaking wet and covered in chills. "What do you mean, *downhill?*"

Terron noticed and grabbed for the go-bag, handing it over to me. "Go get dressed, Ophelia. We're going to be leaving this hotel sooner than I anticipated."

I felt the novelty of meeting up with another advisor's kid wilt dramatically. "But, Terron, we can't just—"

He turned fast, making me flinch. "Get dressed. Now."

I retreated to the bathroom in defeat. "Okay."

I slipped into a new outfit, a loose white dress I would never wear unless I absolutely had to. Why did I pack this and not something more comfortable and practical? I brushed my long hair and tried to untangle it, hearing them argue in the bedroom.

"She has a right to be scared, we all do, but it doesn't mean we ignore the realm we came from when it needs us. Jull is weak, it's the perfect time to strike and—"

"Enough, Sig!" Terron snapped. "I vowed to protect her, not to fight the entire forces under Jull's control to take back over some realm whose population never wanted her to exist in the first place. It's completely ironic for you, of all people, to suggest such a brain-dead idea. Why should we save Isla, and how is she going to be of any use in doing so?"

"She will be powerful. Jull knows it!"

"She's going to stay alive, and that's my sole purpose," Terron said firmly. "You want to play *war*, then go for it. I'm too busy trying to keep her safe from harm, and that includes going anywhere near a denigrating realm."

"You're making a costly mistake. You don't know what's coming, do you?"

I stepped out of the room, half expecting it to be torn apart by the sounds of their bickering. Thankfully, it cut off when I entered the conversation. Terron worked on packing what little we had into the bag, preparing us to leave this roadside motel.

My ankle was still sore, forcing me to limp toward the

bed. As I took a seat on the edge, Sig glanced down at the sight of my twisted ankle and bandaged shoulder. He sat beside me, his lean and calm exterior certainly different from the chubby, spiteful kid I knew growing up.

Terron took the bag outside, only leaving a minute or two before he came back for me.

"I know Isla was difficult for you," Sig hummed. "You weren't exactly treated fairly because of your birthright and you being a female. I understand if you resent Isla—"

"It was my father's biggest responsibility, looking after Isla," I cut in, "he loved our realm, and he tried to protect it, even during his last days. Sometimes, I felt like he loved Isla more than he loved me, but I don't resent it, Sig. I would hate if anything worse were to happen to Isla, but Jull is too dangerous to go against."

Sig leaned back on his hands, crossing his ankles casually. "What if you weren't the only one going against him?"

I eyed the door, waiting for it to swing open. "Terron would never allow it."

"Last I checked," Sig practically sang, "if we were to all assume our fathers' positions, you would overrule Terron. Which means if you wanted to protect Isla, you could do so easily, with a simple claim of your title."

I shuddered at the mention of facing Jull. It was equally horrible to imagine my father's most prized position being ruled over another year, or another minute, by a psycho-pathic murderer.

"Come on, Ophelia," Terron hummed, holding open the door.

I hesitated to move. Sig smiled wide at my silent protest.

Terron spoke lower. "Now, Ophelia. We're leaving."

After everything Isla put me through, I should have left with Terron.

Instead, I stayed.

THROWING A FIT

I've known Terron Matthews since I was old enough to walk. Our innocent friendship turned protective when we fled Isla, and since then, our friendship has been rather strict. I couldn't handle arguing with Terron, and normally I would tuck my tail and move on in an effort to avoid a rather uncomfortable spat with a man I treated as my brother.

With sibling love came sibling fights. This was no exception.

I dodged the table lamp promptly, watching it fly across the hotel room and shatter against the back wall where I paced. I had hoped being back here would deter them from dragging me out of the room, but it looked like I'd only made myself a moving target for tacky hotel amenities. The coffee pot flies next, denting the windowsill.

"Get to the car now, Ophelia. I don't have the patience for this."

"Come on," I begged with Sig sitting nearby, watching this ordeal unfold. "I want to talk to him about a few things, Terron. My mind isn't made up or anything. I'm curious."

"Be curious in the car," Terron snapped. "I'm not letting you declare war on that murderer! He killed the most powerful people in Isla and overthrew an entire realm, Ophelia. I won't sit here and entertain a past childhood tormentor about trying to take back what will never be ours again!"

I flinched. I hated when he screamed. It reminded me of the day we fled. He was screaming for me to run and get out of the capitol, and I'd never run so fast. He held my hand the entire way down the hall, even while the chaos and gunshots continued behind us. I was terrified we would be next, but something about his volatile screams seemed to oddly calm me.

He might have been shouting, but he was focused on keeping me safe. Same as now.

"Listen, I saw a little diner across the street when I came into this Podunk town. Let's go have a cup of coffee and talk through this," Sig suggested, standing between me and the appliance thrower. "Come on, Terron. Let's just go talk things over."

I watched as he finally conceded, waving me over to his side. I wrapped an arm around his bruised back, careful of his wounds, and Sig led us outside. The sun was warm on my skin, shining through my white lace dress. Leaning on Terron, I managed not to limp too terribly on my damaged ankle, spotting the diner across the street buzzing with business.

When we passed the car, Terron went stiff, and I half expected him to throw me into the passenger seat and speed off, blowing off Sig's offer to sit down and talk. Sure enough, his arm caged around my hips, and he pulled me down to the hot asphalt. I tried to push his arm off, but he leveled a hand over my collarbone, shoving me back to the ground.

In my frantic state, I looked sideways, under the car,

seeing a hoard of black boots come rushing our way. I held my breath. Sig ducked down behind a neighboring vehicle, peering under it to meet my gaze. He held his index finger over his lips, trying to keep me silent, but the fear was already written all over my features.

The hunters were here, made obvious by the sight of black boots and black pants with a thin red line down the seam. It brought back too many horrid memories. I choked on the sight, trying to stay quiet.

I watched the boots round the corner, heading for the hallway to our room. Thankfully, none of them stayed outside. Terron took the opportunity to rip the car door open and shove me into the back. Sig jumped into the passenger seat while my Terron started the car and screeched the tires on our way from the parking lot.

Laying down in the backseat, I felt the panic set in, my pulse slamming repeatedly.

"It's okay, we're safe now," Sig said, turning back to calm me down, but it was impossible. I gasped every breath, heaving nonsensically. I grabbed my chest, clawing for my lungs which seemed to have collapsed. Sig turned back to Terron, as the car raced out of town. "We are safe now, right?"

Terron rolled his eyes, and I watched him through the rearview mirror, mumbling profanities under his breath. He spotted my wide, worried eyes and my chest as it heaved with every breath. Something about his stoic and angry exterior softened, and he nodded at me as if giving me a promise we both knew he couldn't keep.

"We will be fine," Terron said, more so to me. "You're going to the first bus stop I find in this state, and our time together is over," he added, shooting Sig a stern glance.

Sig pouted. "I'm starting to think your disdain for me is personal."

Terron was busy assessing our surroundings, his skillset coming in full display as he made sure we weren't being followed as we sped down the desert highway. "Of course, it's personal," he barked. "We couldn't trust you when we were innocent children; you think we should trust you now? You show up randomly from another realm at the same time as Jull's soldiers chase us out of our home."

"You aren't seriously blaming me for that, are you?"

Terron only stared ahead at the road.

"Stop arguing, please," I cut in, trying to ease the tension. "No one is—is at fault!"

"Catch your breath and relax," Terron snapped, giving me a harsh look through the mirror. "You're going into another manic frenzy, and it never ends well. Think of happier things."

As much as I would have loved to, I couldn't settle my racing mind long enough to touch the surface of *calming down*. Everything was hot, achingly so, and the world was passing me by in colors. I had one more day until my special birthday when I got my gift—if I got one at all.

The fear of such an event happening and my gift never appearing was on my mind too much for my pulse to slow. Terron knew it, too, I'm sure. He was probably filling my head with dreams of my gift, which would never come to fruition. It only sent my body into a faster tremble. The ache of my wounds and the palpitation in my heart grew worse with time.

"What happens if she doesn't calm down?" Sig pondered aloud. "You said it never ends well. What do you mean?"

"She has flashbacks of that day," he muttered in reply, driving recklessly through whatever town in Wyoming we were in now. "It haunts her mind so bad that she goes into a comatose state like she's frozen in time or something. I can't get her to snap out of it—she just *does*."

I reeled in the memory of those times, waking up in a hot sweat and drenched in nothing more than pure and utter fear. I didn't think I moved in the first hours since escaping the state of turmoil, but I couldn't let it happen again. I didn't want to fight my mind while fighting Jull's combatants here on Earth.

When my pulse calmed enough for me to think straight, I eyed the bus stop ahead of the front windshield, watching Terron slow down as if to stop at it. Sig sunk further back into his seat and my stomach flipped, knowing if my mind was ever going to heal, then I needed to at least humor the idea of overthrowing Jull and taking back our home realm.

Someone had to step up. Why shouldn't it be us? We were the ones who *should* be running Isla. There was no one better suited to fill the positions of our fathers.

When the car came to a complete stop, Terron stepped out, going back around to Sig's door, ready to throw him onto the sidewalk. I jumped in the front seat, taking Terron's spot behind the wheel, and clicked the doors to lock. Terron pulled at the handle in time to feel it refute his attempt.

Sig gave me a snickering look of pride. "A riff in the family, huh?"

"Something like that," I admitted, meeting Terron's furious eyes through the window. "I can't let Sig leave," I added, speaking loud enough for him to hear my words through the locked door. "It's the first time another advisor kid has sought us out, Terron! We can't kick him to the curb. Not with Jull's soldiers closing in."

"He is not our problem," Terron growled through his clenched teeth. "Unlock the door, Ophelia. We can't take in every stray off the street. He's of no use to us."

"Not so fast," Sig cut in, clicking the window down a notch, but enough to taunt Terron outside his door. He smiled obnoxiously and continued pleading his case, "I know a place we can hide out that's perfectly safe for us. Jull's combatants won't be able to find us there."

Terron offered a skeptical look. "Where would that be, exactly?"

"I can't give up my saving grace," Sig snickered. "Get in the car, and I can drive us out there. It's not far from Cheyenne, so you can always return to the city. But last I heard, your little apartment was ransacked in an attempt to catch our girl."

Terron leaned forward, glaring narrowly through the cracked window. "First off, she's not your anything. She's my responsibility like she has been for the last handful of years. Secondly, Sig, if you think about double-crossing us on this little road trip to a hideout, I'll put a bullet in your neck like you're no better than Jull himself. Got it?"

Sig saluted Terron obnoxiously, trying to tempt him further in frustration, but thankfully, it didn't do too much to set my bodyguard off further. I opened the locks to the doors and got out, letting Sig move over behind the wheel while I circled to the passenger side. Terron held the door open, his hand snatching my wrist before I could duck into the back-seat again.

"If anything goes wrong, you run, Ophelia. I don't trust him, and neither should you."

I only nodded, taking his warning with sympathy for his strategy and skill. When we were all settled into our seats again, Sig pounded the gas pedal, and the car skidded from the bus stop. I tamed my nerves for the rest of the drive, counting my breaths and relaxing my body while the excitement of the last two days combed over me.

With my eyes shut, I imagined that the men up front assumed I'd fallen asleep. Or at least, they talked amongst one another like that was their impression.

"I know she's important to you," Sig pointed out in a

modest whisper, the car humming louder than he was. I strained to listen closer. "You're allowed to be protective, but at a certain point, she's going to have to do something about Isla."

"The realm abandoned her," he growled. "I wouldn't blame her if she wanted to live the rest of her days hoping Isla burns to a crisp. You know all about her suffering there. You caused some of the pain, Sig. Why do you get to offer redemption for a land which wanted her to believe she was a *mistake?*"

"Because no matter what gift she gets, she will use it to free our realm, Terron. I know it's hard to imagine forgiveness for a land, for our people, for me—but if she doesn't get over the past, there will be no future for Isla. Besides, you have to see what's going on out there. They want her now—more than ever before. Everyone does."

Terron shifted in his seat as though glancing back to make sure I was still unconscious, though I was far from it. "Who are you referring to when you say *everyone?*"

"The other advisor kids. There are three others who I've already spoken to about this feat. They're ready to fight, and all we had to do was find you and Ophelia, but given your strategist edge, it's taken us a while to get to you. I searched Topree for a year trying to find her."

"We left there when we could live here without being questioned about parents or jobs. I've gotten by in lifting social security cards and falsifying documents to make me her guardian here. Plus, it gave me an opportunity to have a job while Ophelia could do as she pleased. She was happy before Jull sent his goons after us yesterday."

"Was she?"

The car was silent, and I wanted to answer—no, I wanted to scream it! I deserved happiness and peace, but I also didn't want a safe life knowing the people of Isla suffered. Sure, I could storm the capital there and overthrow the sniveling little dictator once and for all, but I would be hopeless alone. Knowing Sig and the others were prepared for this battle already gave me hope.

That's the only weapon I needed in a war, but a talent for my nineteenth birthday would have been nice too. I fell asleep, dreaming I would get the most amazing, powerful gift possible, and I could use it to overpower Jull once and for all!

I knew it was inconceivably impractical.

COLD FRONT

erron brushes my shoulder with a thickly knit blanket. I turned over, no longer feeling stifled by the short backseat of his fast car. I thought he bought it to be cool and fit in with the realm here, but I was sure it was all in his strategy for fast getaways and reckless movements on the road. None of it outsmarted Sig from finding us.

I was happy for that, at least.

"Terron," I grumbled, clinging to the soft mattress I didn't recall putting myself in. His heavy hand rested on my arm while I turned over again, letting my eyes crease open in slight awareness. "Where—Where are we?"

"A cabin in the middle of nowhere," he breathed, shaking his head. "Sig said we would wait for one of the other advisor kids to arrive, but it's nearly midnight. Nothing yet."

I sat up instantly, feeling my body pop upright in utter shock. "Wait, midnight? So it's almost my birthday then, right?" He only nodded, wiping his narrow, grayish eyes. He brushed his palm through his messy dark hair that needed a wash and slumped forward in exhaustion. "Do you honestly think I'll get a power? I wasn't supposed to be born, Terron. What if I'm what the people of Isla said? A mistake?"

"Power or no power," he growled, "you can be and do whatever you want. Got it?" When I nodded, he pulled the blanket off my hips and collapsed into the bed where I lay. "I'm going to nap since you're already so awake. Don't go outside, don't talk to Sig, and stay close in case something happens."

I could argue with his overbearing rules, but he fell asleep before I could even begin. Besides, I wasn't planning on going outside, anyway. There was no telling how Jull was hunting for me, and the last thing I wanted to do is give him an edge.

I stalked into the living room, shutting the bedroom door behind me. The walls were a light wood material with splintering boards and crooked window frames. The space was small, not nearly large enough for the three of us, let alone more if Sig was correct about us meeting with another advisor kid.

He sat on the leather couch, flipping through a magazine under candlelight. It was apparent this cabin didn't have electricity, a deep difference to the lavish apartment Terron and I had in Cheyenne. In that apartment, the bathtub had jets, and the ceilings were vaulted.

This was a far cry from comfort and luxury.

"Well, look who is awake," Sig hummed, pushing the magazine aside and patting on the couch next to him. "Looks like you got some good rest back there, Ophelia. You knocked out pretty fast. I was worried you wouldn't wake up again until your birthday."

"I think Terron needed the nap more than me," I admitted.

His distant, algae-colored irises fell over me at once, but he didn't seem worried about me right now. Somehow, I could tell he was considering the riff he held with my Terron. They weren't close growing up, and Sig's treatment of me never helped. But this was a time of coming together and fighting a preexisting war, not creating new ones.

"What do you think your power is going to be?" he asked at last. "Maybe something cool, like your bodyguard in there. A mind game of strategy and statistics running through such a small pea brain."

I elbowed his side accordingly and his muffled chuckles slowed to a sluggish halt. "Be nice, Sig. Without his approval, I wouldn't be here. I may have pushed his hand before in the car, but he could have torn you from the seat and went against what I wanted. He's a good guy, a cautious one, but he wants what is best for me."

Sig surrendered at last. "Yeah, I know it. I like giving him a hard time. But seriously, do you have an inclination on what your power might be?"

I shook my head. "No. Did you have a feeling what you would get before yours came through?" I pondered aloud.

I figured it would be a good introduction to know what power Sig possessed after all. I didn't know for sure what any of the advisor kids had, but I could only imagine it was the same as their fathers'. My father was a mind-reader, and while it would be a cool power, I wished it would be something more exciting. We weren't guaranteed our father's gifts, so I could only cross my fingers and hope for something else.

"I'm a techy," he said with a lazy shrug. "I can tamper with anything electrical or runs off a power grid."

My eyes widened in shock. "Wow, that's actually super cool! I guess it doesn't help you out here, though. Doesn't seem to be a cord in this cabin."

"There's not. I checked. Twice."

I stifled a chuckle, watching the arms on the clock over the hall slowly tick closer and closer to midnight. It must have been a windup clock. Time pretty much was the same in all realms. It was a matter of the position of the planet in accordance with the sun, and this time zone linked perfectly with Isla's.

This meant I should get my gift in under two minutes.

"So," I hummed, trying to focus on anything else. "Whose place is this, anyway?"

"Matteo's," he grumbled, rolling his eyes. "The brute strength advisor kid with too much muscle and not enough lights upstairs." He fumbled with his hands in his lap like he was bored of not having an electrical current to toy with. "I don't hate the guy, but he likes to go on those long overnight hunting trips when we could be doing something more productive."

"I'm starving," I admitted. "If he's hunting something good, I'll thank him for it."

"I saw a few ingredients in the kitchen. I can go make us something to nibble on before he comes back. Shouldn't be long now."

I nodded in agreement and watched him duck around the corner. I knew I promised Terron not to go outside, but I caught a glimpse of the dark rolling plains out the window, and it tempted me far too much. I pushed the front door open a little, feeling the warm breeze caress my body. I'd been too wrapped up in my world to stop and gaze at the stars. Maybe I'd feel closer to home.

And it might be what I needed to help my gift come through.

There were millions of diamonds shimmering overhead, illuminating the vast landscape in nothing but moonlight and flecks of stars. It was so awe inspiring and astounding to see, the best sight I'd witnessed since being on Earth, but it was also so humbling.

Isla was out there somewhere. Maybe they were looking

toward the sky as well, lightyears away, and seeing Earth in the far distance. I closed my eyes and pictured my parents watching me from there as if they were still alive—as if they weren't fighting for my existence to be accepted.

There was a sudden chill crawling down my spine, and I hit the gritty dirt, writhing in the dunes of fine sand. I opened my mouth and screamed silently, fighting a pain ripping through every bone in my body until I was left in a shivering, sniffling state. I wiped my cheeks dry when I could feel my limbs again, noticing the tears on my wrist weren't normal drops of water.

I flicked my fingertip against the biggest drop, watching it fly away like a stray fleck of hail from a fresh blizzard. I shot upright from the ground, my heart pounding in my chest when the realization of my power came into play.

Holding my wrist out, I trembled as I forced it forward, watching my ivory skin crawl with snowflakes of ice that encased the surface as much as I demanded. I released the hold on my power, and it melted into drops of cool, fresh water puddling at my feet. I stared at it in horror.

Not only was my power the rarest of them all, a temperament of ice and a creation of an element right from my fingertips, but it was something I'd only seen in one other person before—and it wasn't my father.

I had the same gift as Jull.

BLESSINGS & CURSES

I threw myself back into the cabin, stumbling to stay upright. I caught myself on the couch, and Sig turned the corner curiously, giving me an odd, sideway look with his emerald eyes. I couldn't tell him what power I had, not until I knew for sure it was exactly like Jull's.

If it was, I might be fighting this war for nothing.

Before, the only edge I could have on my opponent was a new power to counter his. Anything at all would help me, but now, all I'd be able to do was fight fire with fire—or in this case, ice with ice. He was more skilled than I was with this power. He'd had it longer! If I told Terron and Sig or any of the other advisor offspring, then they'd deem me useless.

Sig cocked his head while he held the neck of a hot pan in his grip. "Everything okay?"

"Everything is fine." I lied. "A little lightheaded, is all."

His glare flicked to the clock, and his smile widened. "Hey, it's past midnight. You might be able to feel your power, Ophelia. Do you feel anything different?"

I shook my head a little too fast, to the point that I knew it was unconvincing, but he seemed to take it as a nervous reply rather than an untruthful one. He returned back to the fire-lit stovetop and worked over the food on the grates, letting me sink into the couch.

When he brought out two plates of grilled cheese sandwiches, I lost my appetite again, pushing it aside in disinterest. He was far too busy with his growling stomach to acknowledge my refusal and dug into his sandwich. I needed to distract myself from my gift, but my fingertips were still rattled by the sight of what they could do.

I watched the single, flickering candle wick carefully, turning my wrists over in my lap while I considered if I could make something happen without having to touch it. I thought about ice encapsulating the flame, like a frozen bubble in a winter wonderland.

The fire fizzing out in a heartbeat like it'd been doused with water.

"What's going on?" Sig growled, finding a lighter and flicking a flame against the melted cylinder until the wick finally lit again. He cocked his head at the anomaly, and I was sure I'd been caught, but instead, he looked to the ceiling for the culprit. "Most be a leak in this drafty cabin. I don't know what Matteo was thinking when he built this place, but he obviously isn't a roofer."

"Yeah, that's not good," I panted, surprised I could achieve such a reach of power, let alone not get caught with it. I relaxed a little more and picked up my sandwich, only dropping it seconds later when the front door was kicked open. "Agh!"

"Easy," Sig hushed, resting his hand on my shoulder. The brute in the doorway flung a dead deer onto the doorstop in the most gruesome of manners, blood trickling over his muscular chest and abdomen. "Matteo, brother. Back already?"

"I got two turkeys still out there if you want to help fetch them," Matteo's deep, guttural voice replied.

I sat stunned at his physique, which was nothing like the adolescent body I remembered. I wondered what his birthday was like when he got this kind of gift. Did he wake up one morning torn and shredded in so much muscle that he grew in size and height without warning?

My gift was still worse, but at least it was easier to conceal until I figured out how to tell the others of my unfortunate lottery. I would have been better off with nothing, but if I wanted to be of use in this war to take Isla back, then I had to prove myself. This power wasn't exactly the best to combat Jull.

Matteo crossed his arms over his chest and furrowed his tanned, deep brow. "No greeting from the Head Advisor?"

I waited for a moment until I realized he was speaking to me! "Oh, sorry," I hummed. "I—I'm not used to being called that. I wasn't supposed to—I wasn't going to take my father's role or—"

"That was before the circumstances changed, Ophelia," Sig reminded me. "You're as much a part of this rebellion as anyone if not more. Okay?"

I nodded in agreement and offered Matteo a kind head tilt in lieu of a hug. He was still marked with deer blood and shirtless in a shiny, gleaming sheen of sweat. I wished I could recall his mannerisms in our younger days.

I was always with Terron and only knew Sig because of our unfortunate run-ins.

When I should have been making friends with the other advisor kids, I was being ridiculed and questioned as my father's only offspring. I should have been a boy, I should have been gifted better, I should have been the next heir... blah, blah, blah.

Their critiques meant nothing now because no matter if it was harsh, I was not trapped under Jull's reign of unwanted power, and I didn't plan on letting that happen anytime soon.

Special gift or not, I would overcome that director and end this hunt for my life.

Terron popped his head out of the room to see Matteo, and they ran through a brief greeting. I sank into his side when he sat beside me, his warmth comforting when my surface was still cold to the touch. He noticed, pulling a throw off the couch and wrapping me inside of it.

I pulled the edges to my chest and returned to his comforting grasp. "Thank you. I can't seem to warm up right now."

He nodded in understanding. "All good. It's a bit cold in here, anyway. Hopefully, we won't be here long, but I guess I'm not in charge of that kind of move, am I?"

I rolled my eyes at his poking of a power play. He was upset, and rightfully so. He was the group's strategist, and while I should listen to his every suggestion, I was left trusting my instincts instead. While I wouldn't usually be trusted with such a task, we were running short of options after those combatants continued to follow us around.

"Any gift yet?" Terron pondered quietly.

I shook my head, dismissing his question.

He left it at that, probably assuming that I didn't have one after all. Not having a talent would be better than the one I was given. I just wished I could find the strength to admit the truth. I couldn't bear to speak it.

"Hey," Sig called, Matteo poking his head into the dim living room at once. "Where's that old portal of yours? I might be able to reverse the wires and give us a glimpse into Isla."

"You have a portal?" Terron and I asked in unison.

"It's outside in the work shed," Matteo answered with a nonchalant shrug. "It's got a few issues, but you're free to test it out if you want. I haven't been able to jump anywhere yet."

"I came out of Topree in the cave systems in the East of this country," Sig sighed, shaking his head. "The natural portals are so rough and hard on entrance. Having a hand-made portal will certainly help us if we take the fight to Isla. If not, we can still use it to peer through."

"Yeah, but don't those things go both ways? If you make it active, Jull can see that from his end of the realm. He could walk through it and land right at our doorstep," Terron pointed out.

I went taut at such a horrible thought. "I don't want to mess with that thing…"

"I am a whiz at working on portals, guys. It'll be fine," Sig assured us, as even Matteo seemed a little off-put by the idea. "Let me work my magic, and we can go from there. It's going to be harmless. Promise."

I watched them leave, the living room empty now except for me and Terron. He looked over me thoughtfully, my shivering frame wrapped in a blanket that wasn't helping the insatiable chill. He probably thought I was sick, but in reality, it was a bit of ice coursing through every vein in my body, threatening to kill me at a moment's notice.

I pushed away from that morbid thought, wanting to escape his glare while I felt like he could see right through me. If he knew I was hiding something, it would only start a fight. I couldn't have that right now, not on the cusp of a battle I was so ill-prepared for.

Tiptoeing toward the shed outside, I poked my head between the parted doors and spotted Sig as he tinkered with a large metal circle on a platform stand. It was not a huge machine, but tall enough for the likes of me to walk through without ducking. The guys here at the cabin wouldn't be as lucky.

When Terron and I left Topree as older teenagers, we used all the gold pieces we had to use the portal. It sent us to a reciprocal portal in middle America, but it was so long ago that Terron and I probably couldn't point it out on a map. Sig said he used the natural portal in the caves to the East, but that had a one-in-a-million shot of working and not ending up sticking us in the rocks or obliterating us on entry.

He was luckier than he realized.

"If you're going to sneak around and gawk, you may as well come in," he breathed, laboring over a metal switch-board by the arch.

I finally gave in, coming forward to admire the portal that could take us home—if only there wasn't a murderous dictator waiting to wring my neck on the other side. Other than that, it was a simple and magnificent thrill of a ride. It shot our bodies through time and space, letting us land on the only other inhabitable planets in its path.

Isla and Topree.

"So, how does this work?" I muttered curiously. "We're going to be able to see inside?"

"Yeah, that's the idea. We will look inside and see what's there. They won't be able to see us, though, and it won't be open enough for them to travel through. I'm creating a window, Ophelia. Not a door."

I rocked back on my heels with interest, waiting patiently while he flicked around the machine for a while. He eventually pressed his palm to the controls, and the arch lit up, sending an array of colors to morph and align at once, creating a crystal-clear picture of the man who killed my father in cold blood.

I shrieked, tripping off the platform and struggling with balance on my hurt ankle. I hit my side in a gruff cry, trembling as Jull looked directly through the portal with the same grey eyes I recalled from the past. He looked through me specifically, a curiously mysterious smile folding up his cold, callous lips.

"Turn it off!"

WAGING WARS

*T*erron ripped into the shed as soon as the scream pulled from the depths of my throat. He knelt with me, ready to fire off a million questions, but he didn't get to. His focus trailed toward the man on the image of the portal, all while Sig struggled to shut it off. I wept into my arms and turned my back on the man that murdered my father.

Sig finally gasped in relief, and the shed fell dark again, and he returned to the cool and calm man I knew he was. I sat up, my ribs sore and my body creaking in a dim ache. Terron brushed my hair back, shooting Sig a warning look over my shoulder.

"What was that?" Terron snapped. "You could have sent that asshole right into our front yard! He knows where we are now, dammit! There will be combatants here in under an hour, and you—"

"Relax, tough guy," Sig grumbled, rolling his eyes. "It was only a glimpse from our side of the portal. He doesn't know we used it, and he can't see us. I know he can't, okay? It was a bad coincidence that he was in the same room as the portal in Isla."

I trembled, holding myself tightly. "So, he didn't see us?"

"No, we're safe, Ophelia, I promise. I wouldn't put us in that position," Sig replied, allowing calm to return to the shed.

As soon as I thought we were safe, Matteo pushed the door open and gave us all a worried look. His brows were knit, and his eyes widened, all while he sported a new couple of white strands through his dark hair.

"We have a problem."

Terron pulled me to a stand and shivered with his already-spiked rage. "Of course we do. What is it now? More combatants, the world is imploding—oh, let me guess. It's—" Terron stopped as he made it outside first, staring up at the sky overhead. "What the?"

Sig came outside with me, and the cold air of the night licked at us instantly. I shivered at the sheer drop in temperature in just a few minutes. It was cold before, but now it felt like it was below freezing. Small flakes of snow fell from the sky, covering the ground where we stood.

This wasn't a normal blizzard.

My hands tightened at my sides, and I took a cautious step backward. All of the guys were still standing and looking up at the sky in awe. I could feel the ebb and flow of power in my bloodstream, the cold chill traveling through my body and leaking from the sky above us.

While there was plenty of room out here for a blizzard to occur, it was only taking up enough space to engulf the house and the shed in white powder. As for the rest of the ground? Bone dry. If there was ever a worse way to prove my new power, this would be it. I ran into the house, my heart racing out of my chest while my hands slowly began to freeze over.

I couldn't let them see it… I couldn't let them know!

Climbing into the bathroom tub, my hands shook too much to be able to pull my clothes off. Instead, I flipped on the hot shower water and let it slap me instantly. A bellowing scream echoed from my lips while the hot water singed my frozen, snowflake-caked clothes and skin.

By the time the ice melted, the doorway was stuffed with Terron and Sig, leaving Matteo to peer over both of them from the hallway. The steam was oozing off of my skin, and I could tell how crazy I must appear to them. No one spoke. No one moved. Until Sig flicked the pile of fresh snow off his shoulder.

"Yeah, it's too cold out there for me, too," he sighed, pushing his hands through his disheveled hair. "I didn't think about taking a hot shower with my clothes on, but I get it. How come she gets hot water, but there's no electricity, Matteo?"

He pointed to the small window that faced outside. "I have some pipes running through the hot springs outside. It gets me hot water, but you have to be very careful, Ophelia. That water can come out boiling at times."

Somehow with my newfound gift, I guessed I didn't have to worry about getting too hot.

I blinked through the water at Terron, who shook his head. His bottom lip slipped into his grinding teeth while he looked over my frantic state. I glared down at my ankle, thinking that it would have snapped off mid-run, but instead, it didn't feel sore anymore.

When I pulled the bottom of my pants up, I saw a hard case of ice wrapped securely around the heel of my foot, keeping my ankle sealed in sparkling, clear crystal. I shoved my foot under the water quickly, watching the ice melt, and then twisted my ankle around in small circles.

No pain—no nothing.

Terron was the only one in the doorway when I peered back up in awe, although he didn't share in the amazement of this moment. He didn't see the ice, and he didn't know my power. I wanted to tell him how awesome it was that I could heal myself with this ice, but I would have to admit that my power was the same as Jull's.

I couldn't bring myself to do it.

Terron walked into the bathroom and shut the door behind him, sitting on top of the toilet lid with his hands pressed to his kneecaps. "Are you okay, O?" he asked in an urgent whisper. "You looked pretty scared out there."

"I didn't like seeing Jull," I sighed, shaking all over at the sight of his eyes piercing mine—even if Sig said that was a coincidence. "It reminds me of the day we had to leave Isla. I hate thinking about that day."

"I do too, but," he added, speaking just loud enough to hear over the shower water that drowned me in heat, "I was talking about the snow, Ophelia. You looked like you were seriously frightened. It's nothing to worry about, it has nothing to do with Jull."

I nodded slowly, swallowing his words carefully. "I know it doesn't, but it reminds me of him so much. His power is ice. He could kill us all with that too, and I don't want to know why it was snowing in only our spot."

"Yeah, it's strange," he breathed, "but it's Wyoming. It gets cold out here in the wilderness, and it's a cold front. I wouldn't think too much into it, okay? I will always protect you. You know that, right?"

"I know, Terron. Thank you for that," I said at last, now feeling worse about myself.

I knew it was my fault that there was snow. It had to be because I was freaking out over the portal image, and I still didn't know how to harness my gift and keep it safe inside of me. If I messed up again there could be something worse to go through than a small snowstorm.

What if I got us all killed in a tundra blizzard out there?

I sat under the hot water for as long as I could handle it. Terron offered me a long tee shirt to wear when I got out, mostly because my other clothes were filthy from our hasty escape the other day, and I'd decided to jump in the shower in my outfit from today. I stepped into the shirt that was laced with his masculine, woodsy scent, and it made me feel safe almost instantly.

Sig was outside with Terron on the porch, the two of them talking quietly with one another, but at least this time, it looked amicable. Matteo was in the kitchen with his latest kills, and I decided to join him, his eyes diverting away from my bare legs, though this tee shirt covered my lower thighs and didn't show anything.

"Hey, are you hungry?" he asked, cutting a turkey on the kitchen island. I thought of the sandwich I didn't get to eat due to my shot nerves, but this sight didn't help me feel a pang of hunger return. "I won't serve you raw poultry," he added in a snicker. "I can see the look of horror on your face over this bird, but it's for the stockpile in my freezer."

"Oh, okay," I sighed, happy to hear that. "Yeah, if you have something not bloody, I would like to try that."

He nodded with a hum of laughter and washed the feathers and guts off his hands in the sink. I held my breath, seeing him burn himself on the water that came out of the squeaky pipes.

"Dammit," he barked, drying his hands off at once. "The springs are too hot right now."

"Are you okay?"

"Yeah, it's fine," he grumbled, staring up at me curiously. "If the water is this hot right now, was it like that in the shower? Did you end up burning yourself?"

I looked over myself carefully, knowing that the layers of ice that came and went against my surface acted like a pretty good shell to my delicate skin. I only shook my head and worked my way through the kitchen, aiming to find something to eat. Matteo stopped me, pulling me aside by my elbow.

He was so strong that he only used two fingers to yank me away, ushering me back to the table, where I begrudgingly took a seat. Terron always used to act like I was breakable, too. I felt that was a theme with these three guys, all of whom had tried to always get me to sit down and not worry, even if the task was as simple as making dinner.

"I could cook something, you know," I muttered. "You were in the middle of gutting that—" I paused, wondering if it was a turkey because right now it looked like a roadside vulture, "—that bird."

"I can do several things at once, Head Advisor," he hummed, his back turned toward me still.

I winced, feeling a crash of panic fall over me again. I hated hearing that title, knowing that my father was the last one to have held it correctly, and besides, they were never going to let me ascend to the council. They hated my existence! Why should I give them the benefit of the doubt to not do that to me again when the war was over?

My father's voice rang through my head as I thought about our last full day together. He was taking me through the city to get something sweet and to spend time with me, and I got to see how lovingly the people of Isla cared for him.

Most of them glazed over the fact that I was right there with him, ignoring me outright.

If I ever did get back to Isla and the people there truly wanted me to lead, then I would, but it was nothing I could picture happening soon. Besides, Jull would rather have me killed than assume any kind of power in Isla. If I know him like I thought I did, I'd say he had turned everyone against me, and this was a ruse from the other advisor kids to elicit Terron's help and then sideline me from the fight.

I mean, they wouldn't even let me cook my own dinner.

TWINS

I sat outside when the sun came up, needing to feel the heat kiss my face. My body was still sore and cold from last night, and my constant panic of suffocating in my own avalanche wasn't helping. I stared at my hands longingly, wishing I could turn back time and pick any other gift possible.

My father would hate me if he knew the gift I was granted.

I was no better than Jull, doomed to live a cold and miserable life in this pathetic body. I couldn't defeat the one enemy I had, trapped in his domain where he knew this gift far more than I ever could. While I was tempted to play with the ice right now, I couldn't. There were several sets of eyes on me from inside the house.

I decided to rest in the sunshine, watching the snow on the ground finally melt away into puddles of mud where I lingered. I sat on the wooden, rickety porch, my legs hanging over the edge while my head rested on the railing. The warmth of the wind kept my temperature up enough to protect me from creating another snowstorm.

When I fully drifted away, I arrived somewhere new—somewhere cold again.

I lashed at the arms that held me, and instead, I ended up smacking Terron right across his face. He dropped me into the bed with a wounded grumble, and my body ignited with the sudden fear that I'd been moved.

Ice spread onto my palms, and I panicked, rushing back toward the front door, but instead, I ran right into a set of shoulders. Terron pulled me from my daze on the floor, and I fought him still, closing my fists as the ice trailed further up to my wrists and down to my fingertips. It didn't hurt, but it worried me, especially with two new faces in the house.

"Oh wow," one of them gasped, falling to his knees before me.

I stopped thrashing, Terron swapping out in place behind me with Matteo. His arms pinned me to his warm, carved chest, and I had no power to fight him now, my body still begging for the sun to restrain my power so I didn't have to.

The other unfamiliar man knelt as well, and I hiccupped in shock, going limp in Matteo's arms. The pair of men looked oddly similar, their hair stark black and combed over their pale necks. They both had it tied back in short tails and their eyes—they were each striking and unique.

The man on the right had wild red irises, while the man on the left had gorgeous black eyes. I wanted to assume that had something to do with who they were, but I couldn't tell them apart still. I didn't recognize them as advisor kids!

"Are you calmed down now?" Matteo breathed.

I relaxed my hands, feeling the water drip off my fingertips into melted ice. "Yeah," I groaned, thankful I was able to contain my gift alone for now. "Sorry. I—I had a bad dream."

"Have a great right hook, though," Terron grumbled, holding his chin that was imprinted red with my knuckles. "Next time, I think I'll let you sleep outside."

"Good idea," I replied, finally being released from Matteo. Still, the two guys kneeling didn't move, both of them in identical positions on the ground, on the same crooked knee, watching me anxiously.

"Who are you both?"

"Come on, Ophelia," Sig chanted from the couch. "It's everyone's favorite set of twins."

"I can see that, but I don't remember who they are. I don't think I've ever met you," I admitted, trading looks with their similar faces. They both had sharp, pointed jaws that met at the chin, and high, sleek cheekbones with freckles. "Wait. Are you the—"

"Disaster set," Matteo joked.

Sig cackles a laugh. "Hey, I was thinking the, *undynamic duo*. It has a nice ring to it."

"Not funny," Terron growled, motioning for the guys to stand up but they didn't take their eyes off of me. "O, this is Caspian and Elson. They're the twins that can see the future."

"And the past," the twin with black eyes added. "I'm Elson, I can see the past, highness."

"And I'm Caspian," said the twin with red irises. "I'm the future seer, highness."

"Don't call me that," I panted, shaking my head. "I am no one special, please. I am—"

"Your highness," they both hummed, bringing their heads to a bow.

I gave Sig and Terron a confused look of utter puzzlement. I was no royalty, nor was I anywhere deserving of such a title, and besides, why didn't I remember them? They did look a little younger than the rest of us, easily in their mid-teens, but if that was the case, why did they have their gifts already?

They couldn't have been born seers, right?

"How old are you two?"

"Twenty," they replied.

I was taken aback by such a confession, but still, they could pass for twelve if they tried. I stepped away, accidentally running into Matteo's solid frame behind me. He pulled me to sit in a nearby chair, and Terron gave me a blanket to cover my bare legs. I was still stuck wearing his shirt for now, and given my reckless gift, I would much prefer a ski suit.

"This doesn't make any sense," I whispered to Terron who perched on the arm of my chair. "I don't remember them at all."

"You were young when we had to run away," Terron sighed. "We never hung out with them. It was always you and me." He looked sideways, flicking an unkind sneer toward Sig. "Then there were those who we didn't hang out with that still found ways to torment you."

"Very funny, can't let go of the past, *yadda yadda*," Sig spit in reply. "Come on, twins, get off the floor. She isn't buying the whole 'your highness' bit, so let's talk like normal people here, okay?"

Still, they didn't budge.

Terron elbowed my side gently and motioned toward them with his head. I finally played into their weird need to behave this way. "You're good to get up," I grumbled. "You don't have to kneel. I'm not royalty."

They both popped upright like taut springs.

"If I may," Caspian started, his voice still as firm as before. "You actually are. We have spent the last handful of years in hiding throughout Isla. The time of Jull's attack was terrible, but the people of the realm have begun to revolt."

"They're looking for a new leader, you see," Elson added, taking over the explanation from Caspian. "They have all decided that you are the rightful leader. Your father was the

Head Advisor they all admired so much. They don't care about gender anymore—they want you."

I shook my head in pure denial. "Somehow, I doubt that. We have all six of us right here in this room," I groaned. "We're all going to lead together to defeat Jull."

"And then you will lead," the twins said in mighty unison.

"No, I won't," I growled. "We all will. It has always been that way before. We have always lead and inherited group power from our fathers. I won't take over alone because the realm wants me to. I can't lead alone. I can't defeat Jull alone!"

"Not necessarily," Caspian continued. "I know you can defeat him alone. I've seen it."

I inched back further into my seat, eyeing the front door carefully. Matteo moved over there like he could read my mind, standing in front of it while he gave me a worried look. With the panic brewing under my surface, I knew it was only a matter of time before I'd start another blizzard in broad daylight.

"How much have you both seen about me?"

Caspian raised his hand slightly. "That would be me."

"Have you—"

"Do you know if she gets her gift?" Terron blurted. "She was supposed to get it last night, but it never came. What do you see about that?"

I held my breath as Caspian opened his mouth to reply, "No, I haven't seen that specifically. It's bits and pieces right now. As of a few weeks ago, I saw Jull dead in some valley, surrounded by snow and puddled with blood." He glanced up to meet my wide gaze. "I saw you there, too. You had killed him, but I don't know how."

My body relaxed, and hoped no one noticed it. Terron rested an arm over my shoulder while I wrapped myself up in a cold ball. Sig stood apart from the group, pushing past the twins and escaping out the front door. I gave Matteo a narrow look as he let Sig leave.

"I should go talk to him," I whispered. "He looks upset."

Terron pulled me to sit back down, ignoring Sig's abrupt departure. "Don't worry about him. He's mad that there are other advisor kids here who actually respect you."

"Sig respects me," I grumbled.

"Not all the time, though," Terron replied. "He was horrible to you, Ophelia, and he doesn't feel bad about it."

"He was pretty mean to you, highness," Elson added. "I saw some of it myself," he said, tapping his temple. "He wasn't the nicest guy to us either, but we weren't near the capital when Jull attacked. We didn't get to spend much time with any of you."

I stared at my lap, upset that Sig most likely felt ousted from the group because of how he was as a kid. I couldn't blame him for his treatment of me, he had already been forgiven for that. Besides, it was no different than how everyone else treated me when I was younger. I didn't expect people to start calling me *Highness* right away because they were right.

That title was never supposed to be mine.

Terron escaped to the kitchen for a moment, and I used that opportunity to head for the door. Matteo stopped me, eyeing Terron in the kitchen, who was too busy to notice I got up. I didn't know where this sudden need to keep me indoors had come from, but I didn't like it. Matteo eventually moved, and I scurried outside, searching for Sig.

I peered into the shed to see him tinkering with the portal. I couldn't help but admire his ridged stance, his determined glare, and his pale hair and bright eyes. He found my gaze and waved me forward. I pulled the door shut on my entrance and took a seat on the ground next to him while he played with the metal control board on the stand.

"What's wrong?" I asked, skipping right to the issue. "You and Terron were outside last night talking. It almost looked like you were getting along."

"We weren't," he sighed. "We never will. He hates me over some stupid things I pulled back when we were younger, and there's no changing his mind about it now. He thinks I'm going to jeopardize everything."

"That's not true. You're special, Sig. You got us all out here together. We're going to be able to go home because of you, too. It's a great thing, Sig."

He only shrugged. "I'm just tired of being out here already. I want to get to work on defeating Jull and getting ready to fight. The twins, they have a place where we can all go to prepare ourselves. It will also keep us safe from Jull for the time being."

"Good," I groaned. "When should we leave?"

"Tonight," he said, tapping on the portal buttons and watching the colors align again.

I stood on the platform, waiting to see Jull again, but the room was empty this time. It looked like it had to be in the capital. The walls were sparkling ivory, and the floors were the rawest forms of tile I've ever seen. I enjoyed the nostalgia of the foyer more than I thought I would.

My fingers reached for the warp of color, tempted to climb through and return to the realm I was born to run or born to die for. Sig pulled me back a step or two out of caution, seeing a blue movement travel across the image.

"What was that?"

"Not what—but who," he sighed. "Did you see his face?"

I only shook my head, far too focused on the capital to care about who was roaming through it right now. It was like looking at an old, sentimental picture from the past. I wish I could just hop inside and return there now, but it was not possible.

It was not safe.

"That was so weird," Sig breathed.

"Why? What's wrong? It was probably just a combatant of Jull's."

"No, it can't be. He had a scar across his throat. I've seen it before, but—"

The image flickered, and a deafening *boom* echoed through the halls as the image filled with smoke and chaos. Sig and I were both thrown backwards in the sudden shift of the portal and he scrambled to his feet first, shutting it down once again.

I stared at the cloud of dust and smoke that had sept through the portal wall.

"What was that?" I blasted.

"It was an ally," he sighed. "Someone is going after Jull like us, but he seems to be going about it in a much different way."

CARNIVAL GAMES

*S*tuffing six people into Matteo's truck wasn't an option, and with the portal tucked in the bed of the truck, it really wasn't ideal for any of us to ride together. The twins had their car that they followed Terron and I in. He was back to driving his fast car and happy about it too. Meanwhile, Sig and Matteo were hanging in the very back, slowed down by the weight of the portal.

"How far is this place again?" I grumbled. "I hate car rides..."

"I know you do, but we have to be at the twin's spot by tomorrow morning. It will be safer out there in the woods, we are open to exposure out here and prone to attack. Besides, it has electricity."

Still clinging to a blanket I stole off of Sig's couch. "I need a heater. It's so cold in your truck, too."

"Ophelia, I have the seat warmers on, the dash is blowing at eight-five, and you're back in your clothes again with a blanket over your body, too." He shook his head, gasping as the sweat poured from his temples. "I don't understand how you're still cold. I'm going to have a heat stroke over here."

"Then pull over," I breathed, tracing the small city lights on the window as we passed through in the cover of night. "I'm thirsty and—" I sat up straighter, seeing a large Ferris wheel across town spin and glisten with neon pink lights. "Pull over there!"

"Ophelia, really?" He shook his head, speeding the car up in stiff denial. "I'm not taking us over there. It's not a good idea to be out and about with Jull's combatants still lurking in this realm. If they see you, then—"

"Then we have four other advisors to help us get away," I panted. "Come on. We're going to be stuck in the woods for a month trying to take down the biggest dictator in Isla history, and we can't have thirty minutes of fun at the carnival first. I just need a break from reality for a dew minutes! And some carnival food!"

He sighed under his breath, muttering to himself like a grouchy old man. Eventually, he did pull off the two-lane highway and into the town where he and I had been hiding out for years. I admired the intricate iron sculptures and the string lights that hung over the streets. The buildings were built in desert hues and complimented the patches of green grass in the median well.

"I miss being in Cheyenne."

"I do, too," Terron admitted. "But we can't stay here for long, O. It's not safe."

I jumped out of the car as he rolled it to a stop and Sig was instantly by my side. I couldn't help but gawk at the towering rides and the carnival music throbbing in the background. There was a whiff of popcorn and funnel cake wafting over the field that made my mouth water. "It's so pretty here."

"Why are we stopped?" Matteo asked, stomping up toward Sig and I. "What's wrong?"

"Nothing is wrong," I gleamed, pointing to the carnival.

"Just for thirty minutes," Terron added, standing with his hands in his pockets while he looked over the crowded fair. He detested gatherings, and for good reason, but his strategist's brain was already mapping out emergency action plans, so I wasn't worried. Elson gave him a strained look. "What? I can't say no to her. She wants to have some fun."

"Thank you," I sang, skipping past Terron as I entered the carnival.

Caspian hung to my side while Sig and Matteo lingered a few paces behind us. Then there was Terron and Elson, off doing their own thing, apparently. I couldn't help but stare at Caspian's unique red eyes occasionally, finding them just as mysterious as this carnival. He grinned when I caught myself staring at them while in line for a fun ride.

"Sorry," I groaned. "You are probably used to getting stared at a lot here, huh?"

He shrugged it off, glancing behind us while Sig and Matteo were further down the line than us. "Yeah, I'm used to it, highness. I don't mind when people look at me. Probably just as much as you mind when people always stare at you."

"No one stares at me," I corrected, tucking my hair behind my shoulder. "I'm not special."

"Yes, you are. Immensely." He leaned forward, whispering low into the frame of my ear. "Just like your gift."

I hitched a breath, taking a cautious step back. "How do you—"

"Relax," he grinned. "I have known since I got my gift, highness. I've never told anyone, though. Not even my brother. You know, he will find out in about two weeks because he sees the past. But otherwise, you'll be fine. We won't tell anyone."

"Good," I breathed, trembling slightly. I held my palm out to see the ice had returned in my panic, spreading over my shivering palm. "Dammit. I don't know how to harness it yet."

"You should tell Terron," he muttered. "He's a strategist. He knows how to work around others' gifts. Maybe he can help you learn this one. There's no reason for you not to tell anyone. It's not a bad thing."

"It is to me," I whispered. "If it comes down to Jull and me, he knows the gift more than I do. He'll slaughter me with it. I know he will."

"I saw you defeat him," he replied. "I know there's only half a chance that comes true, but—"

"Wait, what?"

"Only fifty percent of the time do my visions come true, highness," he said with an indifferent shrug. "I thought you knew that. I can't see the future if no one has made up their minds yet. There is still free will. You could decide to run away from this war and leave us all hanging. In that instance, yeah, my vision would be false."

The ice on my palm grew and I shoved my hand in my pocket. I could still feel it tangling with my wrist, creeping slowly up my elbow, and there was no hiding it now. I jumped out of line and sprinted for the bathrooms, only to be caught instantly by a deafening siren that blared overhead. I hit the ground, curled into the tightest ball possible, and let the harsh sound wash over me entirely.

When I was brave enough to open my eyes, the crowd had vanished. It was still nighttime, and the stars were still stunning, but the string lights and the carnival rides were running without operators or attendees.

I stood slowly, feeling patches of ice ignite across my spine, but I still managed to move in rigid, uneasy steps. "Terron!" I screamed, my voice carrying for hundreds of miles without anyone to hear it. "Terron! Sig!"

Still, there was silence.

"Over here, sweetheart," a cool voice called—one I knew well enough to feel the fear instantly bubble in my stomach. "Don't be frightened. I can't kill you here. It would take way too much energy from my seer."

I looked over my shoulder slowly, meeting the dead eyes of a man that should never be allowed to walk this realm, or any other realm, ever again. Jull looked the same, leaning on his lengthy legs and sporting a nice suit with black slacks. He glanced over me thoughtfully, grinning as I came towards him like a deer approaching a hunter.

"Is this—is this real?"

"In some ways, yes," he breathed. "I have a special little seer in Isla, sweetheart. He can put me anywhere, at any time, with whoever I want."

I reached my hand out, coming to feel the fabric on his coat before I leaped back and gasped. "How—what are—how is this—"

"Shh," he hummed, stalking closer. I was too frozen now to move, his hand coming against the base of my throat where he pulled his fingertips up my jaw. His touch settled on my chin, insuring I could only look up at him and his deathly gray eyes. "You look good, Ophelia. You've grown so much since I last saw you playing in that little hallway with Terron Matthews. Now look at you. All grown up, wearing your mother's necklace."

He purposefully reached for my moonstone and I stepped back, clutching it tightly. "Don't touch my necklace, or me. You are nothing but a thief anyways!"

"I've never stolen anything that wasn't meant for me to have, sweetheart," he chuckled with a narrow grin. "That includes you. I may not be able to snag you up right now, but I'll be able to drop in whenever I want and find out where you're hiding." He stopped, looking around the carnival as it continued to run empty. "Seems like a bad time to go play carnival games, huh?"

My fist curled at my hip and I launched forward, aiming right for the side of his face. He caught my wrist without even trying, pushing me to the ground while my hand froze over with a solid sheen of pale ice. His dead eyes were touched by life for a moment, and he smiled wider.

"Well, look at that. I guess you have something of mine now."

I pleaded to use my power, wanting to throw an entire blizzard at his face, but I couldn't get it to spread fast enough. Jull reached down as I struggled to move, encasing myself with cold ice as it endlessly wrapped around my body.

He took ahold of my necklace and ripped it off my neck with a wink. "This is mine now, too. Enjoy figuring out your gift, sweetheart. Hopefully, you can use it by the time I come after you once and for all."

I was yanked from the scene and laid out on the dirt path in the middle of the carnival. There were curious glances coming from everywhere and I hid my face. A set of warm and familiar hands found me at last.

"Come here, girl, I got you," Sig breathed, holding me to his solid chest. "Ophelia, you're freezing cold."

My teeth chattered as I attempted to reply, staring at the fun carnival as it was torn away from me. I just wanted to have one night of fun, one night of no hiding—of no worries! I might be nineteen, but I didn't want to deal with this adult war. I just wanted to be normal, no matter what that might look like.

My frozen fingertips pulled over my chest and I could feel the spot my necklace used to occupy. I thought of my mother before she passed, being the only person to truly believe I was meant for something great. It's too bad she was wrong.

WALLS

*T*erron parked the car at the edge of the woods, grumbling still as he came over and opened my door. I dared to walk, but underneath my jeans there was still a light layer of frozen ice. It was not even wet anymore. It just took over my body as it pleased. I turned my head away from him and he stormed out, still muttering curses as he did so.

"Hey," Sig breathed, poking his head into the car. "How are you doing now? A little better?"

I clung to the blanket but ultimately shook my head. Every joint in my body was masked and I couldn't be sure I'd be able to hide it for long. The sun was daring to come out soon so I could use that to help me, but for now I was stuck.

Sig brushed my hair back gently, his fingertips grazing my cheek as he offered a kind grin in place of my sobering frown. He lifted me from my seat and I sank into his arms, resting my chin on his shoulder while the ice mangled around my skin.

"Do you know what happened yet?" Matteo asked, coming to Sig's side.

"I think she fainted," he whispered, holding me tighter. "She hasn't said anything to me. I don't think she's said anything to Terron either, judging by his temper tantrum."

"What about you, Elson?" Matteo asked. "Can you find out what happened? She was fine one minute and then something snapped. She ran off, fell, and can't talk or move around very well. What can you see?"

"Nothing yet," the dark-eyed twin added from somewhere nearby. "Significant amount of time has to pass before I can tap into people's minds like that. She will probably be better by then, so I wouldn't worry about her."

"She's still freezing cold," Sig whispered. "Her body is like an ice cube."

I winced, and he felt it, pausing briefly before he stepped into the woods. It was even colder in there without the moonlight, but I was at least thankful I didn't have to walk through it at all. Instead, I rested my eyes, waiting until I heard someone finally say we were there.

The guys had other plans, talking amongst themselves endlessly.

"Did she feel okay before she passed out?" Sig asked. "Caspian, you were there with her. What was she saying right before she got spooked? Did she see anything?"

He cleared his throat and mulled over the question for a long moment. I almost assumed he is going to tell them the truth, but he didn't. "I don't know. I think she just got over-whelmed. She has been locked up for so long, trying to lay low, that she got exhausted of the carnival."

"Don't say that like it's a bad thing," Terron bit. "I've been keeping her safe all this time. The first time we pull over and let her have a bit of fun, she gets hurt."

"She isn't hurt. She's just not feeling okay," Sig corrected. "She is safe with us. She just needs some rest."

"There's a bunkhouse near the edge of camp. She can

have that one. It's the most comfortable, anyways. Has the biggest bed," Elson mentioned.

I yawned at the idea of getting some real sleep, but every time my mind neared the edge of sleep, I was pulled back into the reality in front of me. I saw Jull two feet from me, reaching for my necklace and ripping it away.

"Stop here," Elson groaned. "Do you feel that?"

"Feel what?" Matteo mumbled.

Terron growled under his breath. "The temperature dropped."

My eyes flew open, and my hands curled around Sig's shirt. I pushed off of him, but he struggled to keep me against his chest. I finally managed to get set down successfully, and I fought to keep upright. My legs were frozen in most places, and the ice in my bones slowed me down.

Sig caressed my cheek, pulling for me to meet his eyes. "What's wrong? Are you cold?"

I clung to the blanket on my shoulders and shook my head. "I—I—"

"Here, how about everyone go ahead," Caspian breathed. "I'll wait here with her. She is obviously just a little anxious."

Everyone except for Terron continued forward, and I stayed back with Caspian, shaking my head. Terron finally paced a little further away, enough for me to pull up my sleeve. My forearm was ribboned with ice, the sparkling crystals lining my wrists to my elbows.

"That's not good," Caspian whispered. "You need to tell them."

"I can't control it," I mumbled. "There's nothing I can do. I don't want them to think I'm dangerous, either. It just won't go away. I saw him and—"

"You saw him?" Caspian came closer, his red eyes flickering the most elegant shade of crimson. "Highness, you have to tell them what happened. They're going to be worried about you. Besides, if you saw him, that means he has a seer of his own. It's not safe."

"Will he know where I am?"

He gave a brief nod. "Yeah. It's not good. Let's get to camp for now and figure out what to do next, okay? But please, consider telling someone about this. If you can't control it, it could kill you."

I lowered my head and fought my way through the woods. Terron stayed behind Caspian and me, closely watching my every rigid movement. By the time we were out of the woods, the ice had drizzled like a cold sweat down my back. I held the blanket still, unsure when this blizzard would end. Caspian pointed to the watercolor horizon in awe.

"Look at that. It's so beautiful," he hummed.

The sky was painted with pink and orange that rushed over the atmosphere above us. Small wooden cabins were sprinkled through the field in the clearing of the forest. People walked around freely, their faces unfamiliar, but their auras so strangely reminiscent of my home in Isla.

I let the sun wash over me at last, the heat burning away at the ice that fought to stay on my pale skin. When it was gone, I rolled up my sleeves, feeling a sea of eyes piercing in my direction.

I swallowed hard and leaned toward Caspian to ask, "Why is everyone looking at me?"

"Highness, they know who you are. You're the one who will end Jull's reign of Isla," he explained. "This is all the willing rebels we could find before our portal broke. We won't be able to use ours, but Sig brought the one he refreshed. We might be able to get more to join us in the fight."

The reality of this war hit me a little harder than I expected. "I don't want anyone to fight," I admitted. "I mean,

I don't want anyone here to get hurt. They shouldn't look up to me for that, Caspian. I can't even control my own gift, let alone—"

"Over here!" Sig called, waving us toward a log cabin nearby. I paused my words for now, coming to the dark wood cabin with wildflowers spurting from the edge of the baseboards outside. "They have a combatant," Sig said, looking primarily at Terron. "We will see him first, then divvy up the cabins and get some rest. Okay?"

We all nodded, Matteo hanging back with me while everyone else entered first. I hesitated in the doorway, not ready to see the face of a hunter who had been sent to Earth to drag me back to my demise. What if it was all a trap, and he escaped, killing us all in his wake? I panicked with every small possibility, fearful that any of them could suddenly come true.

"It's okay," Matteo sighed, poking his head in before coming back to stand with me. "He's handcuffed in there. If you want to go look, it's completely safe."

"I want her to stay back," Terron barked, pointing at the spot where I stood, like he was telling me I couldn't move. I had no interest in going in there before—but now I did!

I walked into the tight space, meeting the gentle glare of a man who was not much older than me. He had wonderful bright eyes but sported a worried, pinched brow. I couldn't help but notice how pathetic he looked without his black mask, simply chained to a post behind a set of bars.

He was harmless in my eyes.

"Is that Ophelia Marshal?"

I swallowed hard when he said my name, another lump forming in my throat seconds later. "Yeah. That's me. Why do you care? What do you want from me?"

He shook his head, his dark mop of hair greasy and in desperate need of a bath. It was only when I took a single step forward that I could see it was not grime and dirt in his hair; it was blood. I covered my mouth to keep from screaming. I'd never seen a wound like this on anyone before, and the thought of war ending up with outcomes like this only made me more uneasy than before.

"Jull is the one who wants you," the man grumbled. "I didn't even care. I didn't know you at all. Now, all of a sudden, you're this fantastical token that he has to obtain. If the people of Isla didn't cheer your name so much, he probably would have forgotten about you."

"Cheer my name?" I repeated, looking to my group of friends for an answer.

Elson stepped forward first, gazing at me with his black irises. "Highness, you are viewed by the realm as the future Head Advisor still. They cheer your name to prove there will always be a successor, even to a dictator."

I toyed with my bare neck, reaching for a necklace that was no longer there. "I never agreed to be anyone's savior," I reminded him carefully. "I am nothing special. We will obtain Isla as a group. We are all advisor's kids here. We will all ascend."

"Not without you," the hunter chuckled. "You're the only thing taking this petty squabble and turning it into a war. With you, the people of Isla would riot harder. He's told them he has you already, that your execution is planned. That way, he can prove to the whole realm that there is no future Head Advisor. There will be no Ophelia Marshal."

I shivered with his threat, and Terron caught it instantly. He pulled me outside, and I hissed, trying to push his hold off my arm, but he refused. I was just glad the ice had melted. Otherwise, I would have had a very long, difficult conversation with him. He was already upset, too. I didn't need to make that worse.

"That's enough story time for now," he griped. "You need

rest after that episode earlier. If you pass out again, we need to know about it. It could have something to do with Jull."

I wanted to argue, but I couldn't. I already knew the answer to that question, but I couldn't tell him. I couldn't admit what I already knew was true.

Because truth was, it petrified me.

HIGHNESS

$\mathcal{I}$ could stay all day in this new bed if I was allowed to, but of course, someone had to ruin my sleep. Sig pounced into bed beside me, ripping me from my casual dreams, and I hissed in shock. He stretched his arms above his head casually, like he was innocent, but my exhaustion was nothing to be trifled with.

I gave him one hard shove forward, and he smacked the floor with an audible *thump*. "Don't wake me up again," I growled, turning over in my bed once more to catch up on more sleep. "Why are you in here so early, anyway?"

"Because you've been asleep all day," he groaned. "It's almost midnight already. You haven't eaten or drank anything in a long time. You have to go to the dining hall with me. Besides, a bunch of the Isla rebels want to meet you."

"Can't I just meet them later?" I whispered.

He fell back into my bed, and I growled a noise to scare him off. It didn't work. He just played with my hair until I grew too frustrated to deal with him. I finally threw the blanket off and kicked myself out of bed. My body was sore and bruised in every spot where ice had laced my skin. Sig noticed through the long shirt I wore as pajamas and cleared his throat.

"What happened? Those weren't there before, Ophelia."

"They're nothing," I whispered, avoiding his eyes so I couldn't directly lie to him. "It's just some stupid bruises from when I fell at the fair. That's all."

"They're all over the place, though," he countered. When he stood, crossing the room to get a closer look at the marks, I stopped him, holding my hand out in reflex. His eyes widened, and he paused, holding his hands out in mock surrender. "Sorry, sorry. I didn't mean to frighten you or get into your space. I'm just worried about you, that's all."

"You and everyone else," I sighed. "Terron hardly wants to talk to me after the carnival thing, but he won't leave me alone either. I could hear him outside all day on the porch of my cabin, just waiting to—"

"To do what?" Terron's voice piqued, his head pulling into view of my open doorway. "Finish your sentence, Ophelia. Please. Tell me how protecting you has always been my job and how you hate it. Go ahead."

I swallowed the awkwardness of this moment, and Sig did too.

"Never mind," I groaned. "Just forget it."

He turned back around, and Sig gave me a playful look. I rolled my eyes at them both and escaped into the bathroom to change into something that would cover more of my body. I splashed some cool water on my face to help wake me up, but when I glanced down at my fingertips, they blossomed with icicles. It was a little daunting to see but also neat.

I pinched the water in my fingers and played with the ice that formed. I didn't understand how something so interesting and unique was so terrifying to me still. I guess it was because of Jull, but the more I toyed with the water, the simpler my gift felt.

I pushed my thumb to the drain and let the water fill up around my hand. When it was high enough, I tried to draw out the same power it took to build the flakes on my fingertips. The sink turned into a block of ice, and the faucet stopped, cut short by the smooth surface of gentle, silky ice around my hand.

It was harmless.

A knock on the door made me jump, my hand still trapped in the block of ice. I winced, hearing Sig call through the wooden door, "Are you okay? It got quiet in there."

"I'm fine," I lied, struggling to cut my hand free. "I'll be out in a second."

I gave up fighting the block when it was clear the ice wasn't going to give way. I had this power, so I should be able to reverse it… right? Either way, I pressed my free hand to the top of the frozen water line and closed my eyes.

When I panicked, ice formed, so I had to try something else. I slowed my pulse with just a gentle breath. Another inhale. Another exhale. My heart seemed to calm with that, but the ice was still strong. Again, I inhaled and exhaled carefully, calling for the chill in the sink to go away.

Soon, my opposite hand pushed through the surface, and water splashed all over the floor. I jumped back, studying my hand carefully, and seeing the bruise that once sparked my surface was now completely healed.

The sink ran normally again and I shut it off as I left the bathroom.

I grinned wide as I met Sig in the room and he nodded for me to follow. I didn't even look toward Terron with our tension still taut. We walked through the grass and stared at the stars. The valley out here was stunning and untouched by trouble. This couldn't be the place of a war. It was too magnificent to be disturbed.

There was a tall fire in the distance with a scatter of rebels around it, passing food, drinks, and even a couple of lighthearted laughs. It'd been so long since I wasn't afraid of being around a group. I thought that would be something the carnival would be for me, but it wasn't. Jull ruined the moment as usual.

Sig took a seat on the longest log near the fire and patted the spot next to him. As soon as I sat down to look around the bonfire, I could see the others paused, their heads all bowed. It made my stomach churn, but I stood, hoping to ease their stress to bow down, but they persisted.

"Stop, please," I panted, pushing my hands into my pockets. "It's not necessary. I'm nothing special, I promise."

Only one of them looked up, her eyes so kind and innocent for a young woman deciding to be a rebel in a coming war. "You *are*, highness. You're the true Head Advisor."

"Thanks, but please, I don't need to be bowed to or treated differently. I just want this war to end like the rest of you. It's not worth bowing to me for. I can't even fight."

She shook her head. "You may not be ready to fight, but we want to fight for you; to fight for the true successors of the advisors."

Everyone glanced up after that and went back to meandering through dinner. I fell back into my seat on the log, Sig wrapping a supportive arm around my back so I didn't land in the grass. I leaned into his warmth, toying with my fingers while I considered her words.

How had I gone from being the most hated accident in Isla to being the one everyone wanted to fight to have power again? I wish they were all doing this when I was younger instead of screaming about how I should have been killed, but it was nice to know I hadn't been forgotten.

I looked past Sig as someone handed us both a plate of food and a cup of water. Terron still stayed a good pace away, watching me like he was the only one here to protect me. I wished I could sate his anxiety over losing me because I genuinely felt safe here, but he wasn't for this idea in the first place.

He didn't want to meet the others, and I didn't understand why.

"Are you okay?" Sig asked again, a question I'd grown tired of hearing. "You look upset, Ophelia."

"I'm not upset, just stunned," I admitted.

"Well, don't be. Everyone is here to support you. You'll be fine. At the end of this war, we can all go back to our titles and live in Isla once again," he breathed. It was a nice fantasy, but I couldn't be sure if it was true.

What if Jull used his seer to find us here? We could be ambushed at any moment, and the war would end before even starting. There were young people scattered all over the place, and they were looking at me for leadership!

I hadn't even thought about eradicating Jull before he sent hunters after me and Terron, but even then, it wasn't anything I had done. I didn't start this war, and I didn't want to finish it. I didn't want anyone to get killed on my behalf, but they'd all made that choice without me.

Every choice had been made without me.

I eyed the portal carefully, seeing that they had successfully brought out Sig's science project to the field. I took one last bite and marched over to it without warning. Sig and Terron followed me in curiosity, but they couldn't catch me fast enough to stop my intentions.

I pressed the button I'd seen Sig hit twice before, and the colors illuminated through the arch. When the picture settled, there was nothing but a familiar face pacing the room back and forth ever so meticulously.

My body rippled in angst as Jull stood in the foyer with his hunters in all black.

"I need another seer, and soon!" he roared, his volume slapping at me harshly. "That seer is too weak to pull me into another vision with her. I need someone else."

"We're looking, sir, but we have bigger issues. The man who bombed the capital, he's—"

"I will handle him," he snarled, biting his words short.

Sig came to my side and Terron did as well, all three of us watching our enemy crumble in anger. He looked so much older than he had in the vision, like he'd aged overnight with heavy bags under his eyes and deeper wrinkles in his forehead.

He reached into his pocket and held up a stunning moon-stone necklace, fixed with silver flowers around the main jewel. He looked it over with pride and my breath hitched at the sight. Terron noticed, pulling at my shoulder to see it was gone from my neck.

"How did he get that necklace?" he snapped. "What did he do to you at the carnival? It was him, wasn't it?"

I could only shake my head in utter humiliation, watching Jull hold it up for everyone to see. "I didn't think a little girl would be my biggest adversary, and I refuse to let that be so. I need her brought back to me with or without the help of a seer."

"How do we do that, sir?"

"She misses her mother's necklace, doesn't she?" he taunted. "We will have to track her down or just let her come find us. After all, she has something of mine now too."

"What does she have?"

"Little Ophelia has the gift of—"

I slammed my hands onto the red button, practically breaking the portal with my sheer force. I panted at the shocked looks from Sig and Terron, not able to come up with an excuse fast enough to explain my outburst.

I needed to hear Jull's next plan, but I couldn't let them know my gift. Sig seemed persistent, reaching for me to ask if I was okay, but I was not. I was furious and scared, and I was in way over my head. I had no choice but to be frightened.

I had no choice but to run from the truth—so I ran.

BLIZZARD

I ran until I couldn't feel the forest floor on my bare feet anymore. My chest was lurching with every breath, and my hands trembled at my sides while I ducked into the endless forest. I could feel Jull chasing after me, his long fingers extended toward the invisible reins around my neck—dying to reach for me and drag me back to Isla.

I knew he was not out here, that he was not chasing me, but the panic of seeing him threaten to bring me back to my home realm and kill me for the sake of ending a rebellion made my life feel more difficult than it already was.

This was new.

The wind blew toward me, stalling my steps when I was finally alone in the dark, surrounded by quiet and cold. It almost felt safer this way, being hugged by the chilly breeze.

I stopped to catch my breath, melting to my knees in the overgrown brush. The ice had come back to haunt me. Little trails of gentle snowflakes dotted my back and sprouted against the sides of my arms.

I just needed to breathe clearly. This war with Jull wasn't going to calm down anytime soon, and I had to realize that I was being pushed to the front lines as the leader. How could I be a leader of the advisors, the only bloodlines in Isla that obtained powers, and I couldn't even harness my own?

I thought of Jull a lot. He was an advisor once, close to my father, and friendly with my family. I remember he came over once, and while my father's other advisors had all snubbed me, he stopped and visited with me. He was thinner back then, lanky, and youthful, too.

I could still see the bright glint in his eyes as he looked over at me where I sat apart from everyone else. He knelt to my level and pulled his hand out of his coat pocket. I can still feel the electricity that shot through me when he held his palm out and exposed a little snowflake on his palm.

He was freezing to the touch, but the crystal artwork in his hand was so tempting for me. I reached forward and took it into my hands, watching it materialize into something different.

I was so proud to show my father, but he nudged me along, my feet catching and the snowflake breaking and melting through my fingers. I was so upset over something so simple, but my heartbreak wouldn't end there. I went to find Jull again, but he was outside in the marble streets, screaming at the other advisors.

My father heard it, rushed outside to settle things, and I never saw him again until he returned with a vengeance. I thought about that little snowflake forever.

I wiped my face of sweat and tears, hitting nothing but patches of ice that replaced them. My heart dulled in pulse, the ice trailing around my torso until I felt it on every inch of my skin. The feeling of it crawling around my neck was when the panic set in, and I coughed, leaning back as the glimmer of moonlight kissed me.

It was not enough to melt the freeze from my body. I had to do something quickly, feeling it growing thicker and tighter around my limbs. I gritted my teeth and closed my eyes, fighting for it to disappear while raw, unfiltered panic struck my chest.

A scream tore from my mouth, covering the woods and echoing off the mountainsides.

I leaned forward, my hands catching me while I fell into the fresh powder that covered the forest floor. My eyes shot open, seeing nothing but snowy diamonds covering everything in the woods. The trees were wrapped in ice, and the leaves were crystalized inside little ice cocoons.

I lay back in the new snow, my body rid of that ice and stared up at the stars between the frozen tree branches. For a minute, everything was peaceful. The guys were probably freaked out and searching for me. I'd put them out of their misery soon, but for now, this was the most I'd ever felt at home, even if it was just a mound of snow in the woods.

Light steps crossed the dead leaves nearby, and I sat up begrudgingly, sure that it was Terron who most likely had this place completely mapped out in his mind by now.

To my surprise, it was not Terron stalking through the woods. I spotted a dark shadow lingering just outside the circumference of my icy outburst. He was a tall man, muscular but not nearly like Matteo. He had dark hair and a sharp, bowtie smile.

"Look at you, Ice Princess," the man snickered. "You got your gift after all."

I swallowed hard, keeping my arms wrapped around me as he moved closer, coming into a funnel of moonlight. His features were sharp, while his smile was lopsided. Otherwise, he was breathtakingly gorgeous with an angular jaw and soft indentions under his cheekbones.

"Who—who are—" I paused, realizing that I'd seen him somewhere. I sat up on my knees, daring to stand, but I was frozen the minute I realized just where I'd seen him before. "You're the guy who bombed the capital in Isla," I gasped.

He tipped his head sideways. "How do you know about that?"

"I saw it in the portal," I breathed. "You were walking from the lobby, and there was an eruption. I saw the marble crack, and then tonight, Jull mentioned it to the combatants. He said he was going to handle you."

He offered a light, sarcastic chuckle that was throaty and deeper than his voice. "Oh, Jull. That tyrannical tyrant couldn't handle a wet mop."

I traced his face in my mind. "Are you a rebel?" I hummed curiously.

His smile grew more mischievous. "No, I'm not."

"But you attacked the capital in Isla. So, you're not close to Jull."

His eyes brightened with my words. "I wouldn't say that, either."

I managed to make it to my feet. The ice crawled through the trees above me. My nerves were on edge while he glared at my body, his cold eyes circling my ankles that were firmly encased in crystal ice.

"Who are you?"

"You should probably work on your gift, Ice Princess," he sighed heavily, his breath hot on my face. "You're going to need it."

Heavy steps were rustling through the woods, and my strange encounter ended. The man bolted into the tree line, and I turned to watch his quick movements, wondering why he was running even further from the camp. If he was not a rebel and was not with Jull, then who was he?

I watched him until his silhouette was no longer in view, and I didn't know why, but I was tempted to run after him.

Instead, warm and familiar hands latched onto my sides, a heavy coat wrapped around my shoulders.

"What happened here?" Sig barked, his voice coarse. "Hey, Ophelia. Are you okay? You look like you've seen a ghost." He took in the small portion of the woods blitzed in an unnatural blizzard. "What happened?"

"I—I don't know," I lied. "It was already out here."

His hand came to my cheek, and he hissed, retracting his touch as soon as it landed. "Ophelia? Your face is frozen!"

I could only shrug, unsure what else to say. He lifted me out of the snow, my ankles dripping while he carried me from the snowy patch of earth. I squirmed in his grip, wanting to walk, but he kept a tight grasp on my body, pinning me to his chest.

"I can walk," I muttered. "I'm fine, Sig, I just—"

"You're shivering, Ophelia. You just ran away from the camp in a panic and everyone is out looking for you," he snarled. "That was so dangerous. You don't know if Jull's men could be in those woods. What if they had gotten to you before me?"

"I can handle things on my own," I assured him, though it was not very convincing. "Put me down, I'm fine."

He gave in, probably sick of my wriggling. My feet hit the warm, dry grass, and I paced out of the trees, feeling the moon kiss my body while the coat parted down the middle. Sig moved to cover me, trying to pull the coat together again, but he stopped.

"What the..." his knuckles dragged over my stomach and I flinched back a step, seeing that he was suddenly enamored with my stomach. "What happened to you?" he asked. "The bruises—they're—"

"Are they worse?" I muttered, worried that the ice that covered me in the woods had marked me up even more than before. I stared down my stomach and discovered that every spot that once sat there was gone. "Oh, well that's kind of—"

"Ophelia!"

I shivered at Terron's tone, his voice ripping through the valley. He stormed out of camp to come directly before me but his hasty pace was halted. Sig stood between us, pressing a fist into Terron's chest.

"Relax, bodyguard," Sig said. "She's fine."

"She's freezing and barefoot," Terron bit through his locked jaw. "You need to get out of my way. It's my job to look after her and she just put herself, and everyone else, at risk."

"She needed some air," Sig fired back. "She's obviously being suffocated here."

Terron's brows pinched. "What are you saying?"

"I'm saying that you're stressing her out. You were pacing outside her cabin all day and now that she's awake, you're on her heels. You can't give her five minutes alone even when she's with another advisor. It's like you can't let her off your leash."

"Watch it," Terron growled. "It's been my job to protect her for nineteen years and I'm not about to let some nerdy techie tell me how to do my job. Now move."

He sidestepped but Sig did as well, building a wall with his body.

I was already fed up with Sig's prince charming bit. I didn't need them to argue about how I felt or why I ran off. I reached for my necklace that wasn't there anymore, grazing my bare neck while I looked back into the woods, wondering where that mysterious man was at now.

Maybe he could see me. Maybe that's why he was here. If he was going to hurt me, he had the perfect opportunity to do so, but instead, he fled. It didn't make any sense, but I couldn't sit around here all night and wait for answers to fall from the sky.

"...ice and snow, like a blizzard in one spot inside the woods. It didn't make any sense," Sig rambled, his voice coming back into my periphery. I glanced sideways to see him talking to Matteo and Caspian, those red eyes glaring through me. "I don't know what's going on, but it doesn't feel right."

Caspian wanted me to tell the truth, to confess that I had a gift, and it was special and cool—but that was just it. It was not special. Jull had it first, and he had spent two of my lifetimes perfecting it.

Whatever highness or fearless leader these rebels thought I was, wasn't true.

But I was not as helpless as Sig and Terron thought I was, either.

"I'm going to my cabin," I mumbled, giving Sig a nod of thanks. "I'll get your coat back to you soon."

"Keep it, Ophelia," he replied with a grin.

Everyone watched as I walked slowly to my cabin on the edge of camp. There was still a looming feeling of someone watching me, but then again, everyone was staring at me. I stopped on my porch, overlooking the wooded land that faced my cabin.

I knew that strange and attractive man was out there lurking.

Despite our brief encounter, I looked forward to seeing him soon. I knew I'd run into him again. For some reason, he was out here for me, and I would find it out eventually.

RIDGED EDGES

It was impossible to miss how my gift had developed in such a short amount of time. Yesterday, I was capable of producing a small blizzard in the woods. I even healed my bruises with a thin layer of ice. If there was anything else I could do, I was not going to discover it by sitting around the campfire with the other advisor kids.

Terron wasn't talking to me, and avoided Sig at all costs and just hung out with Elson most of the time. They sat opposite of the flames, picking at their plates in tentative silence. Sig nudged me with his elbow, vying for my attention but I stared at my food, uninterested in eating very much.

Matteo and Caspian muttered between each other, filling the space with at least a bit of noise. The rest of the Isla rebels had gone down for the night, the advisors being on the opposite schedule of sleep. I preferred the nighttime, anyways. There were less people who bowed down when I walked by and treated me like some kind of monarch.

77

I set my plate down, practically untouched, and got up from my seat.

Heavy steps came after me while I left the fire. I didn't have to turn around to know who was approaching. For once, it was not Terron. His distance these last few days grew wider and further away from me.

"What do you want, Sig?" I muttered.

He brushed my wrist, begging that I slow down. "Hey, come here. Where are you going? You haven't eaten anything in a long time and I'm worried about you. That snow storm that happened to you in the woods—your bruises were gone afterwards."

"I don't know what happened out there, or why," I replied with a shrug.

I felt bad for lying to him, but there was nothing I could do about it. If I admitted that I had my gift then they'd worry about me more. They would think I was just like Jull, that I could be dangerous like he was, or that I wouldn't be able to overpower him.

The panic returned to my hectic mind and I picked up my pace. Sig refused to give up, though.

"Come back," he pleaded. "Ophelia, will you just—"

We neared a separate campfire that was left over in ash from the rebels that sat around it earlier for dinner. I had to be careful to not walk right into the pit of smoldering coals, feeling a weird sense of calmness come over me when I saw the single, flickering flame inside.

No sooner was Sig begging me to stop, that the fire began licking the sky over our heads. I hissed, dodging away from it and Sig did the same, tackling me sideways into the dirt. The fire roared in our faces, the heat unlike anything I'd ever seen before. It towered towards the stars and danced in methodical, purposeful circles.

"What is—" I gusted.

The fire came down and crashed over the ground like a dam that had been cracked down the middle. Sig and I both hurried to our feet, the flames slicing through to separate us. I backed away from the wall of fire, watching it grow in length and in width.

My instinct pulled me to run, to disappear into the woods while the brightly lit bonfire wreaked havoc between me and the other advisor kids, but I couldn't be sure why. I glanced in a panic towards the trees, noticing the soft pair of cyan eyes that I'd seen before.

The man from the forest was back and I knew that he caused this barricade of heat.

Sig called for me but those eyes in the woods beckoned louder.

I raced towards him at once, feeling the heat grow stronger in my pace until the world went dark again. The light from the vicious fire was gone and the flames had fallen for good. The man in the woods had disappeared as well, racing away from me like a vicious game of cat-and-mouse.

"Hey," I panted, begging for him to slow down. "Wait for me, please. I just want to talk!"

He ran faster, taking a sharp turn into what appeared to be a tunneled cave system. I raced after him, wishing I had some shoes on. The rock walls climbed over me and the tunnels were extensively long, each opening branching from the same mouth of the mountainside.

I had picked the tunnel that was closest, charging through it until I hit the edge of a drop, almost falling forward into the chasm before a stiff hand wrapped into my shirt and yanked me back. I hit the ground hard and smack into the solid floor. A familiar set of eyes narrowed as they focused through me.

"Thank—thank you," I groaned. "I didn't even see the drop and you were running so fast."

79

"So you followed me?" he snarled. "I was trying to get your attention, but I didn't want you to run out here to find me. Now the whole motley crew is going to cut down the forest to come find you and if they find me here too, it's going to be even worse."

"Why? Who are you?"

He held out his hand and I took it, letting him yank me upright. He was just like I remembered him, but he seemed scared, if not at least a little worried. His eyes were darting back and forth from me to the opening of the cave, waiting for something.

"It's a long story," he breathed. His hand came around my arm and he tugged me into another tunnel, leading to a dead end where the light no longer reached. "Can you see me?"

"No," I admitted, somewhat worried about what that meant. "Where are—"

A flicker of light flashed between us and the heat that radiated off of it made me wince. A single flame burned from thin air and flickered with my shocked exhale. The mystery man smiled through the dim, yellow light, holding the flame at the base without a hint of a lighter or match.

"How are you doing that?" I gasped. "You're—you're holding fire."

"I can make it dance too," he snickered, spreading his fingers out and splitting the single flame into five. "It's not a common gift, but it's helpful."

"It's amazing," I admitted, reaching to touch it but I tugged my fingers back when the heat licked my skin dangerously. I curled my hand into a painful fist while the fresh burn fizzled against my fingertips. "Ouch, that wasn't very smart."

He snickered as he replied, "No, it wasn't. But you can fix that."

"Really? How?"

"Use your gift," he said as if it was something I should know. "Your ice, Ophelia. It heals."

"How did you know my name?"

"I'm not a rebel, but I'm certainly not an idiot," he sighed. "I also know a lot about your gift. You should have just gotten it this week, right? How do you not know how it works yet? You've got a posse of advisors out there who think they know everything."

"They don't know one thing," I whispered. "They don't know I got my gift."

His eyes widened in the glinting light of fire between us. "Really, now? That's very unusual for you."

"For me? How would you even know anything about me?"

He offered a crooked, eclectic grin. "I know more than you think, Ice Princess."

"Stop calling me that," I growled. "You haven't even told me your name and yet you get to dance around in the woods and play with our campfires. Now I'm lost in a cave with you and you're allowed to taunt me like this? Maybe I'll tell the guys about you, after all."

His grin widened. "You haven't mentioned our brief encounter from before?"

"No," I admitted sheepishly. "I didn't know what to say."

"So the princess does have secrets."

There's a rough sound of steps ringing through the cave and I went stiff, the stranger latching onto my wrist with his hand that wasn't currently aflame. He pulled me closer, breathing into my hair while his lips grazed my ear.

"My name is Decimus," he admitted in a faint purr. "There's going to be a combatant attack in four days. I wanted to warn you, not steal you away—so run back to your posse."

I wanted to ask questions, but I knew I couldn't. The

steps were nearing and Decimus blew out the candle on his fingertips. I rushed through the cave, staggering through the dark while I tried not to slip, or fall into another hole, finally making it to the mouth of the system.

I ran until I slammed into a warm body, the hands latching around my arms while I staggered to steady my vision in the cool moonlight outside. Terron was furious as he held me close to his chest, his eyes drifting through the caves curiously.

"Who else is in here?" he snarled.

I shook my head, trying to pry free of his grasp but he was relentless. "N—No one."

He gave me a warning look, squeezing my arm tighter than necessary. "Ophelia, please don't lie to me. I know you came out here for a reason and the fire, it—"

He paused, the silence between us growing thicker.

"You know what? Never mind," he grumbled. "Let's get back to camp."

"Okay, but can you let go of my arm first? You're hurting me."

"I'm done running after you," he said, not even attempting to release me. "From now on, you're staying within arm's reach of me. I can't keep letting you put yourself in this position. You're going to get hurt."

I wanted to argue but I could tell by his tone that he was not going to let me get very far in a debate. He pushed me through the woods, glancing back every couple of steps like someone was going to come bolting out after us. Still, we arrived at the camp in one piece, Caspian diving towards us and only then did Terron let my arm go.

I followed him toward my cabin, but Caspian stopped me, his eyes wide and panicked. When Terron kept walking, unaware that we'd stopped, I assessed the soreness of my arm from my Terron's grip.

Sig and the others were looking over the burnt ground where the fire licked the camp recklessly. Still, Caspian couldn't take his eyes off of me.

"What's wrong?" I snarled, his crimson irises starting to bother me while they burned brighter in my direction. "You're looking at me like Terron does, like I just did something horrible."

"No," he whispered, unblinking. "It's about what you're going to do, Ophelia."

My heart lurched into my throat. "What are you talking about? Did you see a vision about me?"

"Yes, I did. It's not good, Ophelia. You have to change your mind."

"What are you talking about? What did you see me do?"

He shook his head, the world stalling for a minute. "You're—You're going to betray us all."

TREACHERY

*I*needed to tell them about my gift, about Decimus and his odd involvement in this war, and I needed to confess that I was scared. I was petrified of the ambush Decimus spoke of. But if I told them about my gift, I had to tell them about the ice in the woods and when I first met Decimus. Then it would lead to his grave warning, no matter if it was true or not. They needed to know it all.

But they all looked through me like I was that child at the round table.

"Tell them," Caspian snarled under his breath.

He nudged me to speak, the fire burning between us all in silence. It had been two days since I met Decimus and I was not sure if he was out there still, but I could feel his eyes on my back. Whether it was in my mind or not, I couldn't be sure why he didn't show himself, but it felt wrong to announce it at dinner.

"Ophelia, please," Caspian groaned. "Say something."

"What are you talking about?" Sig snapped, his voice on edge.

Caspian looked at me, but I kept my lips sealed. He spoke

instead, "I just think things have been a little tense out here lately, and I want to get to the bottom of it."

"Tense is an understatement," Terron grumbled.

"Calm down," Elson pleaded, looking at Terron. "You have been really hard on her lately."

"I've been keeping her alive, dammit! I'm not going to be berated again for doing my job. I was tasked with keeping her safe all of my life, and for what? Half of Isla hated her from day one, and now that they want her, she's running every chance she gets!"

Terron's words hit at my body like the fresh kicks of a whip. I winced at the sting of them, wanting to run off to my cabin, but it would only be playing into his claim. I had to fight back for once, but did it have to be against my own people? Against the advisors whom I'm meant to stand with in this war?

I threw my plate into the fire and hoped it would burn. I eyed the trees.

"Don't do it," Matteo groaned from nearby. "You're just going to make things harder, Ophelia."

"Too late for that," Terron bit.

My hands were trembling in taut fists at my side. I wanted to scream, to just make all of this bickering stop, but nothing would shut them up now. Sig was shouting over the fire at Terron while the twins were taking sides, making the riff even deeper. Matteo decided to just bury his face in his hands.

The fire grew in size, easily a foot taller, and I already know that Decimus was out there, trying to pull for my attention. Everyone was fighting and yelling at one another, just trying to talk over the other.

All I'd ever done was to run away. I ran with Terron when Jull attacked. I ran away from the truth about my gift. I ran away from a confrontation with Sig, and now I was contemplating it again. It was a vicious cycle that I couldn't seem to break.

Until now.

My hands flicked out at my hips, and ice shot through the clearing, covering everything in sight. Fluffy specs of snow trickled from the cloudless sky, and a horrid chill marched up my back and settled around my neck. I didn't attempt to stop it, letting it culminate as it saw fit.

Everyone shut their mouths mid-sentence, a cold hush leaking through the Wyoming woods. I reached for my neck, feeling the ice settle into a simple and delicate necklace of crystal. It felt just like my mother's in size, the touch familiar in my mind since the day it was given to me.

"Enough," I panted.

Everyone was frozen, but thankfully not because of my ice. Their glares were all different but they centered around the same sense of confusion and panic.

"What just happened?" Terron asked, standing from the log to see that ice and snow had taken over the bark around where he was sitting. "Did you—did you do this, O?"

I gave Caspian a helpless look but he nodded firmly in support.

"Yeah, it was me," I admitted. "I—I got my gift, after all."

Sig came to my side, his hands brushing over my collarbone where my icy necklace lay. I swallowed, waiting for him to say something, but to my surprise, I didn't see anger. I saw pain. His brow furrowed and he tucked his bottom lip into his teeth, shaking his head slowly in absolute agony.

"You had it all this time?" Sig whispered. "Why didn't you..."

I watched him turn and walk away, forgetting to finish the end of his sentence, but I didn't need him to. I could already see that I'd hurt him. Matteo gave me a pleading look, running after Sig while Caspian was left at my side. I didn't want to face Terron, but I had to.

He'd been like my older brother all of these years, and he knew everything about me. Now we were thrust into a war he didn't want to be in, and I'd already betrayed his trust. I would have understood if he stormed off with Sig, but he came closer, his hand reaching for my arm.

I flinched, afraid of his temper and his innate controlling demeanor. He didn't mention my wince and just threw his arms around my shoulders, tucking me against his warm chest.

"You should have said something to me," he gasped. "You had no reason to hide this."

"It's the same as Jull's," I whispered.

"I don't care, Ophelia. You're still you. There's nothing we can do about what gift you're given. We just have to let you practice it."

My eyes sank to the fire and I hesitated, watching Elson and Caspian make amends from their recent spat over mine and Terron's heated exchange. Everyone seemed to be on the same page for once, all except for Sig who spoke in hushed volume with Matteo. I knew I'd hurt him as well, but I hoped he could understand my reasoning eventually.

Terron pulled back right as Caspian stood, guiding me to the edge of the fire pit. He beckoned everyone's attention without even saying a word. I cowered at his side.

"That's not all," Caspian announced. "I had a vision."

Elson leaned in, watching his brother carefully. "You did? Why didn't you tell us?"

"Because it wasn't good," he sighed. "It could always change so I don't want anyone to worry. But it involved Ophelia."

I hung my head. He told me already about what he saw, but he never mentioned the specifics on what he physically witnessed when I was betraying them. I didn't know if that was possible while I was at this camp.

Why couldn't war be easy and safe?

"Spit it out," Matteo called, hanging his arm on Sig's shoulder.

Caspian gave me a worried look. "She's—I saw—"

A rustling rang out from the woods, catching everyone's attention. I rolled my eyes, knowing that it was just Decimus loitering out there. I didn't know who he was still, but I know he has something to do with this war. I patted Caspian on the shoulder, and I marched towards the trees, wanting every secret to be told already.

Besides, he seemed relatively harmless. He could have killed me before, but he hadn't tried thus far. He was just making his presence known to me. I was ready to expose him, kicking the nearest bush aside when the rustling halted. I expected to see his sharp features, his slightly cocky grin, and those wonderful gray and blue irises.

"Hey, Dec—"

My jaw fell open, seeing that the man in the woods wasn't that mysterious onlooker at all. This man wore stark black clothes and had on a metal and black mask. My stomach flipped, and I backed up, watching as he rose to his feet and pointed a chrome pistol right at my face.

My words stammered in my mouth but never came out, as Terron's desperate scream behind me filled the valley.

"AMBUSH!"

I backed up a few more steps, watching as a hoard of the combatants leaked from the woods. They pointed their guns and dared to fire. I caught a glimpse of rebels rushing through the camp, coming to the dividing line between good and evil.

Then there was me—trapped between them both with a gift I couldn't control.

I tried to find the eyes of the solider who aimed at me, begging for an ounce of mercy or even a simple flicker of focus so I could run off. Instead, no one moves, guns crossing from both sides and pausing before the valley would erupt into total chaos.

"Please," I begged, shaking my head while ice trailed up my wrists like veins. The combatant didn't move, didn't even flinch, steadying his gun to my throat. "I don't want a fight," I choked out.

"That's not up to you," he whispered. "Jull has beckoned for your return to Isla at once. You will come in surrender, or we will sedate you."

At least the deal still stood that Jull didn't want me to die yet. He was still looking for the chance to kill me with his own hands. For now, I assessed my surroundings. There were rioters on our side, armed to the teeth with pistols, and the Combatants held the same leverage scattered through the thick woods.

I just needed my gift to take care of this, to make it all go away, but something told me it wasn't going to work out that way.

"You need to come with me," he said.

Something in his voice sounded different... nearly familiar.

"Wh—What?"

"Come with me," he repeated, pulling at his mask ever so slightly. I caught a glimpse of his eyes, the stormy blues piercing through me. He spoke lower, taking a lunging step forward and resting the barrel of his gun against my throat. He flicked it at my false, ice necklace. "If you want the real one, you're better off coming with me, Ice Princess."

"I can't leave them," I muttered. "I don't want anyone to get hurt."

"It's too late for that. If you don't make a run for it with me, then the others are going to grab you soon, and unlike myself, they actually work for Jull."

I shook my head, panicked. "How can I trust you?"

"You can't. But if you stay here and stand in the middle of this fight, you'll end up dead, or worse."

I didn't need him to elaborate on what was worse than death. I already knew that if Jull got his hands on me, it was over. He would murder me in the marble streets of Isla. There was nothing I wouldn't do to avoid Jull, but I couldn't be sure if I was any safer with Decimus. How did he know of the ambush, and why was he dressed as a combatant?

What if he was really on Jull's side after all, and this was all an elaborate plan to steal me away?

I took a long step back, seeing his body go tight.

"Don't do this, Ice Princess."

I shuddered at his causal, snarling threat. "I can't trust you…"

Someone fired the first shot and the camp gushed with anarchy. My shoulder went numb first, spreading throughout my blood until I collapsed, struggling to stay conscious. Decimus reached for me and hauled me up in his arms while the night sky closed in on me.

"Should have listened to me the first time," he groaned, retreating into the woods while the feeling in my toes withered. "Let the tranquilizer do its job. It's better than a gunshot wound."

I let my head fall over the crane of his elbow, seeing a blur of gunfire and war blossoming into the valley. I could hardly see the advisors anymore, picking out Terron's panicked, desperate features while he knelt behind a large stump with the others.

"I'm sorry," I hissed. "I'm so—sor—"

CAVE CONVERSATIONS

"*E*asy, Princess."

I grumbled, turning over while I was laid on a hard, damp surface. My wrists fought the ropes that secured them behind my back and my eyes refused to open. That was until I realized they were not closed anymore. It was just dark where I was at.

A flame lit the space up at once, igniting warmth to trail through the breezy cave and make the fire dance on Decimus' fingertips. He ignited an old, metal lamp on the floor, illuminating the space in a pale-yellow glow. I swallowed hard, fighting my wrists that remained tied, though my body still throbbed and ached.

He tossed his mask aside, the metal echoing off the walls and making me cringe. "Sorry," he muttered. "You're going to be a little sensitive as the sedative wears off."

I spoke through my teeth in anger and in muscle weakness from the shot I received. "Why did you hit me with a sedative in the first place?"

"I didn't, I only threatened to," he admitted shamelessly. "Someone else hit you with the dart and it knocked you out. I told you to go with me and we could have avoided all of that, but you're just as stubborn as your buddies at the camp."

I forced myself to sit up, no matter how it made my vision spin. "Wait—the others! Are they okay?"

"I don't know. I was a little preoccupied trying to rescue you off of the enemy lines," he snapped. "I told you there was going to be an ambush, Ophelia. You never even told the others about it!"

"Well, why didn't you tell them?" I barked. "Besides, you said they would be there in three days, not two!"

"It's the fact that I knew they were coming in the first place. You should have warned your buddies to be better prepared. For a bunch of rioters, your crew doesn't know how to fight. There should have been a perimeter patrol."

I shook my head, tugging my wrists that refused to budge from behind my back. "Who are you to tell me what I should do?" I fired back, not letting this enigmatic man off the hook just for saving my ass. Then again, did it count as being saved if he had just tied me up and stuffed me in a cave? "By the way, how did you get that mask and those clothes in the first place? Are you a combatant for Jull?"

His face shadowed in skepticism that I reciprocated. "You don't know anything, do you?"

"I know you let me get shot with a sleeping dart," I breathed. "You practically beckoned me over to the woods and then threatened me! If you let me be, I could have stayed with the other advisors, and I wouldn't be tied up in a cave!"

His glare narrowed in an unruly warning. "Stop yelling at me. I'm trying to help you but I won't hesitate to flip sides."

"What side are you on, then?"

He hesitated. "My own. I'm—Well, I'm doing my own thing right now. Just need time to consider, but when I found out that the combatants were coming to ambush, I tried to warn you. I watched you the last few days since, and you never told them. If I let you hang out in the clearing then the real combatants would have gotten you and killed your friends."

"We have an army," I growled. "We could have taken them."

"You have an uprising," he corrected, leaning back against the tall, stony wall. "You're just trying to act tougher than you really are, and you know it. You have rioters without any formal training against a dictator in Isla who has recruited the worst from Topree's streets. You weren't going to make it out of there unscathed without me."

My breath hitched. He might have a point, but I didn't have to admit that.

"Do you know if the others are okay?"

"I wasn't going to leave you in here alone," he sighed. "The minute those combatants realized that you were gone and we weren't going to their meeting point, then I'm sure they backed off the gunfight. Besides, it's just you they want. Leading you out of there might have saved your friends' lives."

I swallowed his words and struggled not to choke. "I hope you're right about that. They don't deserve to be in the middle of this war."

"They are choosing it," he pointed out. "Last I checked, they found you, didn't they?"

"How did you know that?"

He crossed his ankles out in front of him, struggling to get comfortable in the moist cave. He seemed so harmless, but the ropes on my wrists still worried me. I let a chill of ice rush through my wrists and encase the restraints before I relaxed, feeling the ice melt.

Maybe I could make something sharp and cut through, but I didn't even know how to do that. My power only came out when I was emotionally distraught. Even though I was tied up and rather helpless with this strange man, I didn't feel distraught.

If anything, I was peeved by his boyish smirk.

"I know a lot of things," he said at last. "I have been playing both sides of this war before it even began."

"How is that possible?"

"Because I was happy with my life until Jull ruined it. I was around him a lot, and he went into rants often. I could hear the riots starting to worsen in the streets of Isla, and it was clear that trouble was coming, so I took a field trip and found you and Terron out here."

My brows knitted. "How did you know us? I've never seen you before this week."

"I watched from a distance. I even visited Topree a few times just to see who else was realm jumping. The advisor kids were all scattered until I caught wind of Jull's plan. Then they started to gather, and I returned to Isla to watch the show play out."

"Doesn't look like you could stay away," I growled. "You're on Earth bothering me."

"I saved you," he rephrased. "You're welcome, by the way."

"I am not thanking you for anything until you tell me why I'm tied up and what you're planning on doing with me," I snarled. "You say you saved my life, but I'm your prisoner now."

"That's not the case," he moaned. "I just didn't want you throwing snowballs at me until I explained everything."

"Then explain it!"

He readjusted his hands in his lap, giving me a stern stare down. I swallowed hard and caught my breath in the meantime. My hands were able to rub back and forth while the wet rope frayed. I shut my eyes to focus on the ice around my wrists.

Maybe if I could really dampen them, then I could rip free.

He chuckled lightly at my attempts. "You can't do it, can you?"

I released my taut eyelids and met his cyan jewels. "Can't do what exactly?"

"Call your gift," he remarked. "You can do it in a fit of anger, but you can't make it happen if you're not over-whelmed by emotion."

"I wouldn't say that. Right now, I am incredibly frustrated."

"Doesn't count," he rattled off, rolling his eyes for added insult. "Come on, Ice Princess. Aren't you mad?"

My body shivered at his casual taunt. I leaned back against the cave wall, rubbing my wrists back and forth methodically. I was not scared of Decimus, even if I should be. My gift didn't seem to react the way it did when the other advisors were hounding me and constantly bickering with me.

He was different and my gift sensed that, so nothing came.

"Should I make you mad?" he ponders out loud.

My jaw locked and my body went stiff, but not with ice. "Don't."

He leaned forward, the fire in the lantern jumping as he did, and the cave grew brighter. "Your little friends are all probably dead."

My heart lurched and I choked, my windpipe crushed by simple and raw shock. "Shut—u—up."

"They weren't even slightly prepared for this war. They were so busy keeping you grounded and restricted that they couldn't prepare for a measly combatant ambush. You're just a bunch of children with silver spoons, thinking you got something special because your fathers were high and mighty in Isla. You'll never be your father and you will never take his place in Isla. He didn't even like you, let alone consider handing you this title so you could—"

"SHUT UP!"

The cave walls were covered in ice that exploded from my lower back, my wrists tearing through the damp rope and freeing me at last. I pounced upright, a little dizzy and uncoordinated still, but my legs fought the numbness that washed over me.

Decimus was up as well, his hands curled into fists behind his legs, and I used that to my advantage. I held my palms out, pressing them into his shoulders and watching the snowy extract of my gift fire across his clothes, down his body, until he had to break his boots out of the ice that stuck him to the cave floor.

He fell back unbalanced, rubbing his hands over the ice as it scaled across his body. I adjusted my hands, wanting to make him suffer for his words, and directed the ice to his throat with a simple shift of my hands.

The crystals rang around his neck like a necklace of his own, but I could feel the power surging through me. I knew I could use it to do a lot of damage—that I could harden the ice like a rock over his throat and choke the air right out of his neck.

The new knowledge staggered me. For something meant to be stunning and healing, I was surprised that it could be so ruthless.

"Okay" he spit through his locked jaw. "let it go. The point was made."

"Take it back," I snapped, wordlessly irate with the poorly toned mention of my father.

He wasn't perfect, but to this day, he was the reason I was alive.

"You're—choking—me—"

The longer I remained angry, the worse the pressure became on his throat. I wanted to let it go, to watch it melt and run through the caves so I could check on my friends, but I'd already seen these systems once. I wouldn't make it far in the pitch-dark tunnels before I'd get lost or fall to my peril and death.

His hand stretched out sideways, begging for something, but when I moved forward to caress his neck, hoping to ease the ice around his throat, he whipped the lantern fire sideways. I dodged the stream of orange and yellow, feeling it kiss the back of my arm while I was thrown backward from the sheer heat of it. He centered the flames around his neck, warming the line of ice that clung there.

He choked and coughed while catching his breath, and I didn't do anything but watch. My fingertips rattled with a power I'd never known, and the electricity in my blood was throbbing hotter with every moment that passed before he could fully breath again.

His eyes were bold and dangerous in their cyan shade. I leaned back against the cave wall, tossing the threads of my ropes aside while he steadied himself upright.

"You almost killed me," he grunted between heavy breaths.

I cocked my head sideways, admiring my hands as crystals patched around my palm and my wrist. "That's what you get for baiting me to get mad."

"It's the only way your gift will work," he sighed, trembling in the aftermath of such an encounter. "I've seen it done a hundred times. Your emotions are directly linked to your power and the angrier you get or the more upset you become, the stronger it thrives in your veins."

"How would you know that? You said you were close to Jull, but that would make you one of his combatants or a guard for his tyranny. Yet you sit here and preach that you're a pacifist, a man on both sides of this war—which would make you someone in the middle."

His eyes darkened. "I'm not in the middle by choice. I would join you and your friends if—"

I sat up straighter making him pause, seeing the words catch in his throat that was now licked by blisters from his life-saving gift. "If what? What ties do you have to Jull?"

After a thoughtful pause, he looked away, stealing the sapphires from sight.

"He's my father."

WHAT'S SAID IN THE DARK

*I*f I knew how to get out of here, I would run. The caves were far too expansive and the darkness was unforgiving. I could use the lantern to make a hasty escape but he controlled the flame. I could get ten feet into the pitch dark, and he could steal that single flickering flame back.

For now, I held my legs to my chest and leaned against the cave wall, watching him lap water from a fresh pool nearby. It dripped from the ceiling like a river flowed over our heads, pressing and poking its way through the cracks until it formed in the dead end of the cave tunnel.

I inched myself closer to his position on the floor, pressing the water to his neck carefully. He hissed when I reached to graze the burns, curious how his gift could be so unforgiving to its host.

"Does it hurt?"

"Not as much as having an ice noose wrapped around my throat," he grated. "I'm used to the burns by now. I've had to go through my own learning process with my gift. It wasn't always easy."

I hesitated probing into a conversation that would poke the surface of his relationship to Jull, but it was really the only thing I could think of that would satisfy my desire to know what led him here. Besides, he admitted that he wanted to join my side of the war.

Would that make him a potential ally or a really obvious mole in our midst? Either way, I pushed my hand past both of his, still toying with the ice on my fingertips. Our skin connected, and he hissed, almost pulling away, but I moved the energy through my knuckles, willing the ice to form with just my determination.

He grumbled under his breath, watching me lean over to graze his neck. He doesn't trust me, and that's fine; I don't have much confidence in him, either.

"Easy, Ice Princess," he snarled, flicking a flame under my chin in warning. I let him use his collateral as he wanted, just hoping he didn't burn my hair off in the midst of making a point. "Awwww," he bit, shivering as the ice circled his neck again. "It's so cold."

"It'll go away soon. Just give me a second."

I thought of the bruises on my body from the first time the ice cracked my surface. I wasn't anticipating it to happen, but it wounded me in my haste and in my overwhelming emotions. It had pressed into my surface, pushing and kneading bruises and welts into my skin.

Then in the woods, while I was alone and erratic, the ice trailed over me in the moonlight and dissolved seconds later, leaving me with a healed body and an intact mind. It was freeing for me, though I was not so sure Decimus was happy with the same experience. He kept his threat of fire on my neck alive while I let the ice trickle off his neck in the form of simple cold water.

I brushed my hand across his cool neck while the burns

that once licked his skin disappeared. He retracted his fire away from me by dipping his hands into the water before patting them curiously along his neck. His eyes widened when he didn't feel the cool sheen of my gift anymore.

"The burns," he gusted. "They're actually—"

"I healed them," I whispered. "Isn't that great?"

"It's—I don't understand," he groaned, sitting back next to the puddle while I did the same to face him. He moved his hands around his neck again to pull out some kind of answer, but there really wasn't one. "How did you do that, exactly?"

"I don't know," I admitted with a modest shrug. "I had bruises on my body before I ran into the woods, and you found me in the snow. When Sig found me and brought me back to camp, the bruises were gone."

His eyes were illuminated in the dark. "Yeah, that's different."

"What do you mean? Can—" My words stopped before saying the name, not wanting to utter it out loud but knowing I had to. He knew the most about my nemesis and it was more than some caged combatant at camp could ever tell us. "Could Jull do that?"

He shook his head at my poignant question. "Not that I could recall," he sighed. "I've never seen something like that. My fire would never have that effect, let alone has Jull ever used his gift to heal someone."

I perked up. Maybe it was an advantage, but in the same breath, could it really be an advantage? After all, what was I going to do on the battle field if I faced Jull head on?

Heal him to death?

Highly doubtful.

I relaxed my hands and ran them through my scalp, tussling with my messy, greasy hair while I tried to think of other things. The cave walls were tight enough, I didn't need to suffocate myself in stress over what this could mean.

Maybe I was not like Jull at all. It was a distant reach of a child's dream, but it could be true. It could mean that I was more powerful than him! But I'd seen his work at play, and I didn't think it was a struggle to figure out who had the advantage with this gift.

He was making snowflakes in his hands when I was just a baby. I couldn't make that happen now if I tried. Besides that, I was stuck in this cycle of anger and frustration that was hitting me from every angle now. It was the only way my gift came of any use.

I imploded on myself in the woods. I blew up the valley into a winter wonderland when Terron berated me in front of the others. Then there was Decimus who looked at me with a clear sense of amazement. He had only made me mad to trigger my anger—my power. While I admired his dedication to pissing me off to prove a point, it hadn't gotten me far.

All I had so far was the inclined ability to drop the temperature when I was angry.

I blocked out the memory of choking Decimus with my gift. The mere thought of that kind of power made my bones ache. I was not a murderer, and I was not a monster, either.

I was just confused.

"When can I go back to my friends?" I muttered at last, my voice hardly even bouncing off the cave walls.

"We have to wait until the combatants leave the area. They're going to either think I took you to Jull and retreat to their portal so they can get home, or they will know I've taken you and go searching."

I shook my head at both options. "Either way, we're screwed."

"Why do you say that?"

"Because when Jull finds out eventually that I'm not with the others, he will come looking for me. How do we even know where their portal is? What if it's right outside of camp, and he could come through at any moment?" I shuddered and forced myself to a stand, eyeing the tunnel ahead. "I have to go be with the others. I can protect them."

"No, you can't," he said simply.

I remained unflinchingly still, hearing his words echo off the back of my head. "Wh—what did you just say? You saw what I did to you, Decimus, so it's clear I have a powerful gift."

"They would never let you protect them, sweetheart."

I winced at his casual pet name, but it was a lot better than the one he'd been using for me. I let it slide for now and turned to face him, watching his emotionless features as he toyed with a flame in his lap, tossing it from palm to palm like it was a ball.

"Why do you say that?" I prodded.

He flashed a smile. "Because you're just the face of revolution. The one everyone fights for, but not the one they fight alongside. You can have the rebels bowing as you pass by and the people of Isla would never talk about how they really felt about you in the past because you're just an idea."

"An idea? I am the daughter of—"

"Oh, don't start with all that posturing, I don't want to hear it," he growled through his gritted teeth. "You're the daughter of the Head Advisor that died over a decade ago. You're the woman everyone sees as a return to normalcy—to as normal as things can get in Isla, but you will never be their general of war, Ophelia. You're their precious jewel they stuff in a box, shove into a desk, and forget about until it's time to tote you back out again."

My stomach ached with his claim, unsure if that was truly what was going on here or not.

I couldn't trust a word that he said. He was the enemy's son and he hadn't made his intentions clear just yet on what he planned on doing with me next.

"Don't you see it?" he asked, cocking his brows up as he watched me stammer in place. "They hinder your every move because they see you as unfit and ill-prepared for battle."

"That was because they thought I didn't get my gift," I griped. "Plus, they were just protecting me. Terron has been doing it since I was young, it's his sole job to look after me. It's not like I walk into minefields every day and require guidance to get out of them."

"Really now?" he said, skepticism heavy in his tone. "If I remember correctly, you did come to the woods when you heard me messing around, right?"

"In the ambush, yeah, I did, but—"

"But nothing," he bit, shooting to his feet and throwing his flame into oblivion. "You were two inches from getting shot in the neck and if it was any other combatant that caught your attention first, you would have been dead."

"I knew it was you, though," I fired back. "I knew that you—"

"You know nothing!" He screamed now, taking two lunging steps until we were chest to chest in this cave. He settled his rattled breath to continue. "You're the little girl no one has ever believed in. You will remain that little girl if you allow those guys to run this war for you."

"They're not running it for me," I bit.

"Really? So you sought out Sig in the city? You found Matteo and the twins by what, your ingenuous strategy? You had this camp and those rebels here because you thought that far ahead? Or has every choice up to this point been about keeping you on the sidelines so you could smile and fuel the fire of war?"

I swallowed his words carefully, a lump building in my throat. "Are you saying I'm just a pawn, then?"

His grin widened. "Oh, sweetheart. You're not even on the chessboard."

FEVER DREAMS

I had every intention of smacking that stupid and smug smile off of Decimus' lips. He crossed his arms against his chest and widened his grin with delight, looking over me for a reaction. I tried not to give him one, to not let this devil win, but he'd proven his point and it was hard to argue with.

I looked at his throat like I might have to freeze it again, but there was something else that caught my eye. Just under his jawline was an old, faded scar. I didn't even notice it before, but somehow it looked so familiar.

"Where did you get that cut?" I asked, shaking my head slowly. "It should have healed when I fixed the burns on your neck."

He brushed the spot thoughtfully, already aware of what I was talking about. "It was put there with an enchanted blade. There's no fixing it. Not even with your gift."

"Why is it there?" I breathed. "Who did that to you?"

He looked aside for a moment, seemingly calmed down from our spat. "My father tried to kill me. He did the same with my mother, so we wouldn't face retaliation if he died in the capitol the day he slaughtered the advisors. I lived. My mother didn't."

I winced at such a horrible thing for a man to do to his son. Especially since he was just an innocent child in Jull's master scheme to ruin my life and kill my father.

The mere thought of Jull trying to slit Decimus' throat made me Ill for some reason. And his poor mother—

My hand curled over my stomach, and I winced, backing away from him at last. I inhaled sharply, a painful sensation growing over my body that sent me to my knees. Decimus was beside me in seconds, his hand resting lightly on my lower back while I leaned forward, nearly ready to hurl everything that might still be in my stomach onto the cave floor.

"Agh," I whimpered, doubling over to my side and curling into a tight, throbbing ball of ache. "It—hurts—"

"Easy, princess, I have you," Decimus whispered, pulling my shirt up where I fought to keep my arms pressed into my stomach. He hissed a noise in abrupt shock. "You're doing it to yourself."

My eyes were wet with tears that I prayed wouldn't freeze to my eyelids, but I was not sure how my power even worked at this point. He cradled the back of my head and pulled me forward so I could see the ice that covered my stomach and my sides. I didn't even feel the cold before, but I did now, watching spikes and ridged edges form against the surface.

"Oh, no," I panted, trembling as the ice flared around my body, crawling up to my chest and coming for my neck. "I can't stop it," I pleaded, utterly shaking with angst. "It's just—it won't stop!"

"Dammit," Decimus snapped, ripping his shirt off. He lay down on the cave floor and inched my shirt up, nearly over my bare chest, before I stopped him. "What are you doing?

You're going to freeze to death if you don't let me help you!" he yelled.

"My shirt," I whined, the ice making its way to my neck. "I don't have anything on underneath it. I don't want you to see me—" I choked, the ice lacing a trail up to my chin and fighting to suffocate me slowly.

"You don't have time for modesty," he growled.

Decimus yanked my shirt completely off and pulled me to his chest. His arms wrapped firmly against my back, and he pinned me to his bare torso, holding his breath while his skin started to heat up by will. I hissed at the fiery surface of his body, needing to break away, but he squeezed me far too tight for me to back off.

He cradled my head against his bicep, using the gift in his warm bloodstream to melt the ice as it formed. It worked so well that I began to sweat, panting to breathe as it felt as if I'd been locked inside a sauna.

I coughed slightly, a bit of ice water coming up my lungs and freezing against my bottom lip. My head fell back in exhaustion, and I whined slightly, the ice on my mouth starting to grow every time I thought of Decimus calling me a lowly *pawn*.

"Hey, now. Stay with me," he hummed, eyeing me carefully. His eyes dropped to my lips, overrun with fresh ice. He dared to pull his hand off my back, and I winced, trying to yank myself away and cover my bare chest that was still pinned to his body, but he snaked his arms back into place. "So feisty," he groaned. "You made this choice, not me."

He leaned forward, pressing his lips to mine. I almost squirmed in shock, but truthfully, he was gentle, his lips burning in more ways than one. I found myself leaning into his body, my fingertips tentatively massaging into his chest muscles before he pulled his lips back and gusted in ache.

"Your fingertips," he grated, speaking through his clenched teeth.

I paused, looking over his chest to see I'd built tiny snowflakes across his warm skin. He fought to melt them off and I watched him carefully, wondering if he would kiss me again. He simply looked over me, clinging to my body while I curled against his bare warmth.

"You've got to get a handle on this," he sighed at last, letting his temple rest on the cave floor. "Your ice is starting to get out of control. You'll end up killing yourself or someone else in the crosshairs."

"I wouldn't do that," I muttered. "I can control it enough to keep me safe, I know that I can. I was just so angry about what you said and—and I'm not all that great with my emotions, anyways."

"Yeah, I can tell," he grumbled. "We have all had traumatic things happen, princess. You can't let it weigh you down and blame every fleeting ounce of anger you have on it. It's just going to drown you; or in this case, turn us both into popsicles."

I shuddered at the thought. "If you know how, then tell me. But I can't just make it stop. It doesn't work like that."

"I wish I had all the answers, Ophelia."

I inched back slightly, surprised that he used my real name this time. For the longest stretch of my childhood, no one would call me by my name. I was the unwanted, the forgotten, and the utterly hated. Now, with even the son of my enemy holding me to keep me alive, hearing my name brought me a sense of self again.

I went limp in his arms for the first time and he noticed me relax.

"What?" he asked, his hands loosening around my sides. "Why are you looking at me like that?"

"Because for once, you didn't say my name like you hated me."

"I don't hate you," he said firmly. "I never said I hated you. I might ruffle your feathers a little bit and get on your nerves, but you do the same to me."

"Yeah, but you seek me out," I affirmed. "The moment in the woods when you came across me before. Then again when you were playing with our campfire. You wanted my attention. You seek me out every time and still, you refuse to tell me whose side you're really on."

"I'll end up on the winning side," he said with a sneering smile.

I rolled my eyes. "You don't know that. You can't be on the winning side if you haven't chosen who you will fight for yet. You are Jull's son. You have the added pressure of pleasing your father. But you also did attack the capital at one point, so I know you're not working for him right now."

He rolled his eyes, pulling one of his hands forward so he could brush my cheek. He pushed my hair back, feeling the cool tone of my skin that withered into warmth with his touch. He was keeping me intact and thawed for now. I wanted to thank him but I couldn't, dying to know who this enigmatic man would fight for in the end.

"I want to be on your side," he sighed. "but it's not that simple."

"Why not?"

He shook his head, pulling his hand back away from my cheek. "Because if I choose to fight for your side fully, it wouldn't work so well."

"I don't think that's true," I said. "You're powerful in your gift, Decimus. The others would love to have you on our—"

"I almost killed Sig."

My heart leaped into my throat, and I pushed him away from me, stalking my eyes over his exhausted features while I tried to tame my fear. The ice formed in patches on my back, but he couldn't see them. Instead, he watched me clasp my arms around my bare chest while he sat up slowly, his hands out in forfeit.

He stared at the ground by my feet, my toes cold and nearly blue in color. I ignored the ice that snaked across my surface, fighting to regulate my punching heart as it nearly ripped through my chest and fell on the floor between us.

"You didn't," I said, shaking my head. "When? Why?"

"It was a misunderstanding," he growled. "I told you I went realm-hopping for a bit after the riots started getting a little out of hand for my father. While I was in Topree, I ran into Sig. He must have heard about Jull's talks to kill you or whatever, and he thought I was there to hurt him." Decimus clenched his eyes shut as if reliving the moment.

I shook my head, hoping that this was all a major misunderstanding. "Go on."

"I just wanted to talk to him about what was coming, but he lived in this techy nightmare of a house that was rigged with all sorts of machines and wiring. He ran inside, and I went after him, triggering a boobytrap that ended up sending a spike toward my chest." He paused, inhaling slowly while he caught his breath. "I lit the place on fire while he was still inside."

My throat lurched with pressure, and I gagged onto the floor nearby, the anxiety of the situation overwhelming me once and for all. While bent over on my knees, I groaned and shook, Decimus inching closer when I flinched away from his looming touch.

"You're doing it again," he groaned, placing his hand on my lower back. "You're going to freeze to death, and I won't be able to save you eventually."

I hissed in an effort to get his touch off of me, but he ignored me outright, yanking me onto my side and curling his chest around my bare back, pinning me against him yet again. At least this way, I didn't have to see his face right now. I just let the warmth of his torso line my spine in heat.

"You almost killed him," I growled, shivering in my pathetic state. "How could you?"

"It wasn't intentional. He started it, dammit. I was just trying to talk to him. I had to do something."

"You should have left us alone," I spat out. "*All* of us."

For the first time, his touch went cold. "Really? That's how you feel?"

Truthfully, no. He got on my nerves, but he did undoubtedly save my life. He even tried to warn me before the attack, and I didn't listen. Instead, I thought I could handle things on my own. I wanted to be the leader that everyone thought I was, but maybe he was right. Maybe I was not even fit to be the general of this war, let alone the Head Advisor of Isla.

I was completely stuck, and I didn't know what to do.

"No," I said, speaking the solemn truth. "That's not how I feel."

His hands were looped around my sides and pressed against my stomach. They began to flicker with a light warmth. It felt comforting. "Good," he said. "Because I care about you, princess. I've just tried to be honest, and I had to be honest here about Sig. I would join your side if I thought it would be safe, but the others will never accept me."

I shook my head, leaning back slightly. "They will if I tell them to."

"You haven't been listening to me at all, have you?"

I swallowed the lump in my throat and finally turned over in his arms, letting him hold me without caring what he saw or didn't see.

"I know you think that they have been stifling me or that I haven't been a good leader of this rebellion, but I'm trying to be better. The rioters want to follow me back to Isla. They want me as the leader. That's all that matters in the end, not the opinions of the other advisors."

He tipped his head down ever so slightly, and his warm exhale pushed across my cheek. "Are you so sure about that, Ophelia? They hate me. They will never accept me. They don't want me on their side of the war."

"I want you," I admitted softly.

His eyes widened, their vivid color making my body flush with heat. "How exactly do you want me?"

Without any other words to prove how I felt, I communicated the only way I knew how. I pushed my lips onto his. He didn't hesitate to reciprocate, his hands curling around my sides while pulling me tight against him.

He flipped his body over mine, and I lay on my back, wrapping my arms loosely around his warm bare shoulders. When he paused for a breath, I bit my lip.

I stared at the scar on his throat, transfixed with the brutality of it, while he sat up and paused our kiss.

"Should we be doing this?" he groaned. "I just told you that I almost killed one of your friends. I can't be on your side when this war comes, Ophelia."

I pulled him back over me, his lips grazing mine as I said, "You didn't kill him. Because you're a good guy. They will see that, Decimus. I know they will because I can see you are good. You're not your father."

His gaze turned to fire, and his mouth dipped to take mine. I lay back and enjoyed the bliss of this moment, all the while knowing that there was nothing my friends could do to stop Decimus from helping us defeat Jull. In his own weird way of showing it, I knew Decimus cared about me, and he didn't want to see me lose this fight.

Even in war, there needs to be a bit of love.

RETURN

$\mathcal{I}$ woke up on the cave floor, alone but thankfully warm.

A blanket had been tucked around my body, and I was curled in a ball next to a kindling fire that dwindled in front of me. I reached for Decimus, wanting to find him with me still, but the space was empty.

Beside the small fire was a note and a poorly drawn picture on the other side as I peeled it open to read.

It looked like it was scribbled on some spare piece of trash he found in the Wyoming woods, and he used some kind of charcoal rock to write it, but I knew it was from Decimus just by the first line.

Hey, Ice Princess.

Sorry I had to leave you like this. I am on your side, but they will never accept me like you have. I know you think that you can handle this battle, but it's not that simple. Nothing is. Go back to camp and get ready for my father's return. He will come for you.

Be safe, Ophelia. War is imminent. Don't forget that I care about you.

Yours, Decimus.

I felt the urge to cry over the stupid note, turning it over to see that he had drawn a map of the cave systems and shown me a way out. I snatched the lantern still burning nearby and followed his instructions completely. But I stopped and took one last look at that small grotto. I would always remember it and the special kisses.

Sunlight brimmed at the edge of the cave system, and I heard voices outside. I paused, wondering if it could be the combatants, but when I heard a familiar deep yell, I knew it to be otherwise.

"Ophelia!"

I dropped the lantern and stuffed the note into my back pocket, flinging myself into Terron's arms. He caught me instantly, gasping in shock while he kept me locked in his fierce hold. I wept into his shoulder, taking in the strong scent of his woodsy smell.

"Ophelia," he growled, fighting through his frustrations while he squeezed me nearly to death. "I've been so worried about you. I thought for sure you were gone and in Isla already. We were about to send the rebels into the portal so we could kill Jull earlier and get you back."

I whimpered against his shoulder, my feet finally touching the soft grass. He smiled wearily as he wiped my tears away, brushing them aside while he looked me over. I could tell already that he was looking for wounds, but I didn't have any. I just had relief that my best friend, the closest person I had to a brother, had found me first.

"Where are the others?" I gasped, falling into his embrace once more. "Are they okay? The combatants, they were going to kill—"

"Everyone is safe and alive," he assured me, running his hand across my back methodically. "We fought them off, and they retreated early. We knew when that soldier took you that they had gotten what they wanted, but when they left, we couldn't find them anymore. We couldn't find *you*."

"I've been safe this whole time," I gusted. "Everything is fine. I just want to get back to camp."

Terron looked as if he wanted to get to the bottom of where I'd been, but my stomach growled at the smells lingering from the camp. I had to hold my gut and winced, starving for something, anything, after however long Decimus had kept me in that cave to protect me—and more.

He should be returning to the camp with me now, but he had made his choice.

He chose to leave my side in this war. Maybe he didn't care about me as much as he said he did. Either way, I couldn't argue with him about it now. He was gone. Terron helped me find my way back to camp, and I spied Sig first, watching him run towards me with his arms out.

My feet left the ground again as I was sucked into an embrace that could have broken my ribs. He put me down, and the cycle continued through all of the advisor kids—all except Elson. I looked to Caspian who seemed overjoyed to have me back, letting him wrap me up in another hug.

"I'm so happy you're back."

"I am too," I hummed. "Where is your brother?"

He snapped back, his arms falling while he looked to the others for an answer. Everyone seemed hesitant to reply, Terron taking me aside with a hand pressed to my shoulder. I watched as the others tried to comfort Caspian, but there was nothing positive on their defeated faces.

"What's wrong? Is he okay?"

Terron pulled me to my cabin and hesitated on the front porch. "There was an incident after you left camp. In the middle of the battle, we sort of lost sight of Elson for a moment."

I pressed my fingertips to my lips. "Oh no, did he get wounded in battle?"

"Do you remember when Jull said he needed another seer to help him find out where we were? And then the combatants got here not that long after we heard him through the portal?"

"Yeah, of course I do," I gusted.

"Well, he had inside help."

I shook my head as ice trailed around my ankles, freezing me to the porch. "No, he couldn't have. He was the one who helped get this place started, Terron! Why would he turn on us like that?"

"He wasn't turning on us," Caspian sighed, unknowingly lingering near the edge of my cabin. "He was turning on you, highness."

I fell back into the rocking chair, wanting to escape back into the woods and find Decimus for his help. He seemed to know everything about this war and I was left playing catch up. How was it even fair that the man who respected me the most, aside from his brother, and treated me like I was some kind of royalty would sell me out to Jull?

Why would he want any of us hurt or killed? It didn't make sense.

"I don't—" I hissed, trying to relax but the ice on my body wasn't fond of this discussion. "I don't understand why."

"Because he saw the vision that I had seen before," Caspian muttered, leaning on the railing of the porch while Terron stayed back a few steps, watching the brother very closely. "He woke me up the night before the ambush to talk about what he saw."

"I still don't know what vision you had that would make it seem like I would betray any of you," I gusted. "I wouldn't do that. I want to defeat Jull as much as the rest of you."

Terron cleared his through, pulling my focus. "But what about Decimus?"

I swallowed the name carefully and tried not to react. "What about who?"

Caspian's face fell in disapproval. "Highness, please. Don't make this worse."

I traded a look between them both, needing to know what they knew so I didn't end up screwing myself in the end. Besides that, I didn't want them to think I would ever betray them. They pushed me out in front of this war! Why would I ruin it now?

Caspian continued when it was clear I wouldn't speak about Jull's son. "I didn't know Elson could see my vision so I couldn't get another one in time to learn what his plan was. He decided at the last minute to sell you out and give Jull the information he needed to find us."

I shook my head. "He tried to get everyone killed?"

Again, there was a stagnant pause.

"Not exactly," Terron breathed. "The soldiers pretty much gave up the minute you were out of sight. They retreated before we could even put up a decent fight and make them surrender. It all happened so fast. We think the deal was that if Elson gave you up to Jull, then no one else would get hurt."

"But Isla would lose the war if I died," I snapped. "He would kill me and the riots would end. They wouldn't care about winning anymore. That's what Jull wants! How could Elson think that I would want Jull to win, that I would betray anyone for that fate?"

"Again, you're missing something, highness."

I buried my face into my hands with nothing but pure confusion and unease. "Then please, just tell me what has happened. Just tell me everything that you saw in your vision that would make me out to be a villain. What did I do to deserve Elson turning on just me?"

"It's not Elson that betrayed us," Terron sighed. "It's you. Caspian, just tell her already, please. I can't stand here much longer and not know if it's true or not."

I stared into those crimson irises with nothing but turmoil surging through my veins. He shook his head, running a hand through his hair while he steadied his nerves. I could only assume that they were as on fire as mine were.

"I saw a vision of you and Decimus, highness. You two had been kissing and confessed some kind of feelings for one another."

I froze, unsure why that was a bad thing...

His words didn't elicit betrayal in my eyes but he seemed to read them differently.

"So, is it true?" Terron probed. "Did you do that? Do you care about him?"

I hesitated to answer and looked frantically between them both.

"If I did, why does that mean I betrayed anyone?"

Caspian turned his back to me and Terron held a hand over his face in utter angst. I still waited for a reply, for an explanation, but no one was willing to give me one. Instead, I looked to the woods that faced my cabin, wondering if Decimus was out there watching me.

If he was, I hoped he didn't know that he was right about my friends.

They did hate him with everything they've got and now they might hate me too.

SUBDUE

erron pulled me from the rocking chair and shoved me inside the cabin. He attempted to close the door, but I panicked, pressing it back open and shoving my wrist in the way. He wouldn't hurt me and I could see the frustration in his eyes as I fought him.

"Just talk to me, please," I begged. "Why does it matter what I've done with Decimus? It doesn't mean I want to betray anyone! I want this war to end with us ahead of it, Terron!"

He shook his head and pinned the door against my wrist. I yelped and he released the pressure slightly, but not enough for my comfort. "You have feelings for the enemy, Ophelia, can't you see that? I've been trying to protect you from this war for years and you think it's wise to fall for the son of a monster?"

"He isn't on Jull's side!"

Caspian finally came forward, shoving Terron aside. The door was yanked open and with my wrist freed, I hit the floor on my knees.

Both men looked over me curiously but Caspian pulled

me off the ground and yanked me over to sit in bed. I stirred uncomfortably, seeing his hand come forward and rest gently against my cheek. He had such smooth, refined fingertips that I couldn't help but relax under his touch.

"This isn't going to hurt you physically," he muttered. "But you need to see the vision I've had. It might be the only thing that can explain this mess for you."

I looked to Terron, still upset over his attitude. He just paced away from the room so he didn't have to look at me much longer. It hurt so much to see him think I'd betray anyone, especially him.

I was the reason he came out here in the first place.

"Fine," I sighed, watching tears fall into my lap and freeze on contact. "Do what you must. I would love to know how you think this is all a betrayal."

Caspian held my face in his hand and closed his eyes, steadying his breathing to a low, gentle pace. I was too tempted to watch his process to copy it, just noticing his body go limp before the sight was swiped away from me once and for all. I thought my body fell forward but I couldn't be sure, blinking to find I was suddenly outside, kneeling in the soft coverage of snow that covered the camp valley.

The other advisors were behind me, but Caspian stood with me, his hand wrapped firmly around my arm. He helped me out of the snow, pointing forward to the dark shadows of the woods. I could feel the trickle of snow sprinkling from the sky, landing on my face as I looked toward whatever he was trying to show me.

"There's nothing there," I said, my breath pouring from my lips in a white cloud.

"Just wait a moment," he urged. His eyes were the brightest ruby shade I'd ever seen before. He stared at the tree line intensely, watching as figures began to emerge into the fresh powdered grass. "There he is."

I squinted slightly recognizing Jull's cold features as he stood in front, adorned all in black with gold studs mimicking metals of honor on his coat. He looked like an advisor, wearing the uniform my father wore every day for decades.

It was purposeful and in poor taste, I knew that much.

"Where is she?" Jull called, his voice booming over the valley. "Bring her to me now!"

He turned around after a moment of silence, reaching into the woods and yanking a man forward. I could tell already that it was Decimus he possessed, his own son drenched in blood and heaving for air as he was thrown into the snow. He was unable to protect himself from the fall while his hands were bound tightly behind his back.

Jull pulled out a pistol and snarled as his voice carried for miles. "Come here to me now, or I'll kill Decimus instead!"

I shake my head in horror, pressing my palm to my lips while tears freeze against my cheek in mortification. "How could he—"

"I'm right here!" A familiar voice screamed in return and the vision went taut with tension.

Caspian squeezed my wrist tighter and I leaned into his side, seeing the vision-version of me race from the camp, running between the two feuding sides. I wanted to reach out and beg her to stop, to rethink this terrible idea, but I kept running closer and closer until Jull got his hands on me.

I stood over Decimus protectively, Jull laughing as he raised the gun to my chest and fired a shot, killing me at once.

My lips parted in a scream while I watched myself fall over Decimus, blood pouring out in excess from my wound. Jull laughed as he toyed with his gun, neglecting the sight of his own son and me while we died at his hands.

Caspian released my wrist at once and I awoke in bed, still screaming at the top of my lungs. He pulled me to sit up, but I was too distraught, too frightened to move, that I could only thrash and shove him away, the sound of my sobs ringing from the back of my throat. He brushed my hair aside and kissed my cheek lightly.

"You see now what you've set yourself up for," he sighed. "I got that vision early this morning. I can only guess that it happened right after you made your choice with Decimus in the cave. You care for him, and that's not a bad thing, but it won't save us in the end."

I sniffled and wiped my tears, launching from the bed and racing off the porch. The minute my feet hit the grass, Terron had caged me in his arms, refusing to let me go. I screamed again, kicking at his legs and punching at his arms, but he didn't release me.

He spoke into my ear as I pushed my head onto his shoulder, needing to pry out of his hold. "You've got to stay put, Ophelia. It's the only way you're going to live."

"I have to find him. I can't let Jull get to him first!"

"You have to forget about him,O! He is the reason you will die!"

I thrashed and writhed harder, screaming until I thought I might lose my voice. "Decimus! Decimus! Please, stay here! He's coming! Decimus!"

"Enough of this tantrum," Terron growled, carrying me back inside the cabin. I grabbed onto the railing, onto anything I could get my hands on, just to prevent being thrown back into bed. I clung to the doorframe and fought him harder, hearing him snarl against my struggling movements. "Dammit, Ophelia, It's for your own good! Do you want to die?"

"I don't want him to get hurt, please!"

"That's the problem," he grunted, finally ripping my

hands from the wooden doorframe. "You're going to give yourself up for that traitor! You have no right to sacrifice yourself for this war. I won't let you do it!"

He was practically screaming in my face as he threw me onto the bed, pushing his knee into my stomach to pin me there while his hand tried to hold my arms. I scratched at his arms endlessly, watching my closest friend, my protector, bleed at my will. He didn't flinch, but just kept me trapped under his hold while muttering something to Caspian.

When he turned back to look at me, I could spy tears in his eyes. It almost made me want to stop, never having seen him cry before. He didn't let up though. He just shook his head and inhaled a slow, steady breath.

"I'm sorry, but I can't let you die," he muttered, his tears streaking down his face.

"If you let me find him, I can stop this before it happens, please!" I gasped, his hand on my shoulders not wounding me, but it was certainly enough to keep me from getting up and charging out of here again. "I don't want him to die, please, Terron! Let me go!"

He looked away from me, biting back a set of sobs that might match mine. I didn't want to hurt him, but he was not leaving me much of a choice anymore. I squeezed my fingers into his wrist, closed my eyes, and let the power surge through me with one final push.

Ice raked up Terron's body and knocked him over with a hard *thump* when he hit the floor. I caught my breath first before rushing out of the cabin, darting straight for the woods. The sooner I found Decimus, the better.

If he was taken by Jull first and then used as bait for my death, then there was nothing I could do to save either of us. I would still sacrifice myself for him. He didn't deserve to be tortured by his own father! I wouldn't allow it.

I made it just outside the trees before thick arms wrapped

around my shoulders. I dared to fire ice up Matteo's grasp, but he kept me still long enough for a sharp needle to jab into the skin of my neck. I winced, screaming out in one last attempt to get Decimus out here, but the sound slowly leaked from my throat until I was silent and limp.

I blinked sideways, Matteo's grasp loosening while I gave up the fight. My eyelids felt heavier than before, the sensation of the world spinning around me started to steal my focus. I wanted them to let me help, to let me fix things before the fight began, but maybe Decimus was right after all. Maybe I was just a pawn.

I was the face of a revolution that I was not allowed to fight in.

I slumped sideways and spied the syringe in someone's grasp. My eyes trailed up the figure while clouds formed in front of my vision as I caught sight of Sig weeping before me. He turned around at once, tossing the bloodied needle aside.

"Take her to her cabin," Sig grunted. "She won't be a casualty in this war. She's too valuable."

I would have laughed at his choice of word for me but I slipped into my unconsciousness before given the chance. *Valuable*, he said. Almost like a precious jewel to be tucked away in a box and shoved into a drawer until it had further use to be toted out for everyone to see.

Valuable and useful had two very different meanings and I knew which one I was to these guys, and which one I'd always wanted to be for Isla.

LUCID DREAMS

"You will get a special gift, one meant for you," my mother said through her typical warm grin. She held me into her side, both of us stuck listening to the beeping of the machine nearby. It hadn't stopped beeping since she arrived here, but she didn't seem to mind it anymore. "Your father has a gift, you know. One that is needed and worthy for him to look over Isla and protect it."

My eyes widened with puerile hope. "Really? What is it, mommy?"

She brushed my cheek with her long nails. "He's a healer, sweetheart. He can take the pain out of anyone."

I felt my brows pinch. "Why can't he heal you?"

"Because it's not meant for me to heal, sweetheart. I asked a seer a long time ago about my moment, about the end of my magnificent life, and he told me exactly how it would go. You know what? I'm okay with it."

I suffered through an inhale, wondering how she could succumb to such a terrible illness and leave me behind. "Why can't daddy just heal you? I don't want you to die, mommy. I don't!"

"Shh, baby. I know you don't. But it's destiny."

We both worked to wipe my tears away, although they were too fast to catch as they lined my face in a matter of seconds. "I don't understand. Why is your destiny to die?"

She smiled through her weary pain. "I don't have the answers but I do know yours is to live, sweetheart. It's just how destiny works. We already know what is to come of this realm, of our family, and we've made our peace with it. We don't know when, exactly, but we know it will be soon."

A cold shiver worked through my body and the tears only came faster. "I don't get it. Why can't you stop it? Don't you want to be with me forever, mommy?"

She nodded, her face paling. "It's just the way it works," she whispered. "If I had the time to explain it, I would, sweetheart. You have to find the world out on your own. If I live, and your father lives, you will just acquire a realm that will reject you. If we let destiny work itself out, then you will come back a hero."

I shook my head. Nothing of her words made any sense anymore. "Just stay with me, please. I don't want you to leave me."

Her eyes glossed over and she moves me forward, kissing my forehead for a long, painful moment until I no longer felt her breath on my skin. I pushed back, seeing her eyes shut and her body frozen in time.

I screamed, my father racing into the room where the machines had all silenced. He picked me up off the bed, setting me on my unsteady legs. He didn't even seem to be upset, nothing touching his stoic face. He brushed my hair back, nudging me out of the room and into the hallway that lacked medical staff.

No one cared that my mother had died!

My father knelt, pulling a chain out of his back pocket and opening his palm to expose a gorgeous blue stone. He worked it over my head without having to undo the clasp, forcing a grin over his lips while he kissed my forehead just as my mother had.

"She would want you to have that," he said in a pained whisper. "She loved you, Ophelia. I love you, too. I just want you to know that none of this is your fault."

I shook my head, dazed over the passing of my mother. "Why couldn't you just heal her? I don't care about me, daddy! I just want you both to be okay."

His smile grew in strength. "Exactly, baby girl. That's why you will outlive us all. You will rule Isla one day and I can only protect you by letting destiny and fate take the reins."

"This world hates me," I muttered. "I'm a mistake."

He scowled at my words, grabbing my little chin in his massive hand turning my face to his. "Listen to me, Ophelia. You are not a mistake. You're the only thing keeping this world together when trouble strikes. I know you don't see it, but I have. You will rule over this land once you get over these aches. Just promise me one thing."

I nodded my head when he dropped his hand. "I'll try."

"Don't hold onto this pain for too long. Your gift will not be fueled with rage. It's powered by love. You just don't see it yet. I've seen it all and I want you to always remember that I'm so proud of you."

He wiped my tears and stood. A set of faces appeared at the end of the hall. My father collected himself better than I could, shaking the hands of an older man and a young boy nearly three times my young age.

My father leveled with that boy next, patting him on his shoulder. "She's yours to protect now. I need you to promise that you will watch over her with everything you've got."

The young boy nodded dutifully. "Yes, sir. I will."

"Good, Terron. You will help her rule one day."

I turned my head in confusion, still so unclear on so

many things that just didn't make sense in my mind. I couldn't ask my father anything. I could only dwell on my pain, on the sadness in my soul. There was nothing to fix anymore. Like my father and mother had both said, everything was decided already.

I pushed this moment away, needing to focus on something else. This wasn't a memory I wanted to keep of my parents. My hand clenched the stone around my neck and I shut my eyes softly. I released this moment forever and vowed never to think of it again.

* * *

I SHOT UP IN BED, covered in a frozen sweat. My body was trembling so hard in the cold that I winced as I moved, realizing that I was not in my bed at all. It was a filthy cot with an audience set up across the room, behind a set of bars that matched the ones in front of me.

"Looks who's awake," the combatant snarled. "I was beginning to think you were dead. You wouldn't stop whimpering and crying for hours and then it just stopped. You've been really annoying to listen to."

I sneered slightly, feeling so stiff and sore as I tried to push out of bed. "Where is everyone?"

"Who? The other prisoners of this war? It's just us, princess."

"Don't call me that!"

He winced with an edge of a grin pulling at his lips. "Oh, someone doesn't like being called that. Alright, Ophelia. I'll play along. You don't remember what happened, do you?"

I clung to the bars, fighting to pull the memory to mind but all I could see was the moment my mother died. I was so young that I thought I made it all up. It still didn't feel real, and neither did my father's words, but I remembered meeting Terron for the first time.

I was just happy to have a friend in my time of mourning.

I didn't know what it would turn into.

Using my cold fingertips, I dragged a light touch over a prick in my neck, flinching at the feeling of Sig jabbing a needle into my throat. I couldn't imagine why he would do such a thing, but then Caspian's vision returned to my head.

My knees knocked and I fought to remain standing, clinging to the bars while I could practically feel the bullet poke into my skin. How this whole betrayal ordeal started was beyond me. I just wanted to be with Decimus. I thought we connected and had something special, but instead I was stuck trying defend why I would sacrifice myself for his life.

They had the right idea trying to subdue me, but if they had just let me go after him, maybe I could have saved Jull's son from meeting a terrible fate.

They had such little faith in me.

"You look pale," the soldier snarled, no longer handcuffed but still as spiteful as the first time I went to talk to him. "Are you sick or something?"

I cocked my head at his rather empathetic tone. "No, why do you say that?"

"Your skin," he hummed. "You're covered in bruises and in blisters. I think while you were passed out, your teeth were chattering. I know it got cold in here for some reason, but you look like it was hitting you a little differently."

I pushed my arms through the bars, taking in the ice that swirled around my skin, hiding deep marks underneath like the last time I got too overwhelmed with Jull and this war. I wanted to heal them but I didn't even have the energy. I counted the number of marks on my surface and lifted my shirt up to see a hard plate of ice against my ribs that drooled with blood that curled down my hip.

"Well, that's not good," I hissed, lowering my shirt.

"How are you doing that?" The combatant backed up slightly like I was some kind of monster. "It's growing in size on your neck."

I felt the ice straining across my skin, crawling up my throat and settling on my cheek. Leaving it be, it trailed around my temple and then crawled through my scalp, twirling around each strand of hair.

It practically encased me and I let it, almost in a final submission to my power.

"Hey!" the combatant screamed, his voice rocking me backward. "We need some help in here!"

I fell onto the cot, letting the ice take over my lips and seep into my mouth. It cooled my sore throat, working to trail all the way into my system, into my blood, and take over my body from the inside out. It was almost cathartic in a sense, feeling my gift take the last thing away from me that I had.

I'd lost my family, I'd lost the friends that I thought cared for me, I'd even lost the man who dared to save me despite knowing that he would never be accepted here.

I couldn't control this gift anymore and I felt like it had already stolen everything it possibly could have from me. It was no gift. It was a detriment. So, why not let it take me too?

I greeted my father and held onto him like I'd never leave his side again.

BACK TO ME

*J*couldn't help but dream about my parents. They loved me too much to deserve the fate that was brought over them. They just wanted to keep me safe, to keep me happy, and they died for me. How could I be so selfish as to squander their sacrifices.

I'm sorry mom.

I lurched forward, met with a steaming hot embrace that collapsed over me. I sunk into the warm skin of the man next to me, unable to make sense of my mind anymore. I could pick up Decimus' scent as he squeezed me tighter, brushing his lips to my cheek.

"You're okay, Ice Princess. I got you now."

I held him tighter at the sound of his voice in my head. His skin warmed me up enough to feel normal again and my eyes opened, afraid the feeling of him would drift away with the feeling of his touch on my body. His eyes were wild, wet, and the purest shade of blue.

He pulled at a smile, pressing his burning hot palm against my cheek. "You look great," he whispered. "Thanks for coming back to me, Ophelia."

I couldn't help but smile. "You said my name."

"I'll say it every minute of the day if it keeps you here with me," he hummed. "Just never let that stupid ice do that to you again. We almost lost you."

My brows furrowed. "Who? My mom and dad?"

His brows furrowed. "No, Ophelia. Everyone. The other advisor kids."

I sat up slightly, peering over his shoulder to see the bars in our way, blocking out Terron, Sig, Caspian, and Matteo. They all gave me a panicked look, like everything that just happened was real. Like I almost died...

I pushed my hand against Decimus' face and he growled slightly, pulling away from me. My breath hitched in shock, unsure how any of this had come about. He sat up next, pulling me sideways into his chest where his heated gift overwhelmed me.

"You are going to be just fine," he added with a kiss against my temple.

"Terron," I sniffled, fighting back more sobs. He had his sleeves rolled up, showing a patch of bruises that I knew came from my ice. "I'm so sorr—"

"Don't apologize, O," he said in heavy exhale, "you did nothing wrong. I should have listened to you from the start."

I gave Sig a pitiful look, recalling how he wept after putting me to sleep. I should have been angry with him, with all of them, but I couldn't find the words to express anything other than being grateful. Then again, I looked at them through bars.

"Why are we still jailed?" I pondered, looking to Decimus.

He scanned the crowed on the other side of the cage. "After you screamed for me, I came after you, thinking there was trouble. They had already sedated you when I made it over here so they pulled me aside to talk. They wanted to make sure I wouldn't pull any tricks so they put you in here in the meantime."

"You were frozen to the cot when the prisoner screamed for help," Matteo sighed.

The combatant raised his head slightly, with sadness in his eyes. I couldn't determine why but I pitied the man terribly. This cell was so cramped and uncomfortable, and the anger in his eyes fled while he looked at me with guilt.

"I did the best I could to bring you back. I can't believe it worked," Decimus added, kissing my shoulder. "You can't do that again. Your gift is off limits."

I stared at the floor next, processing my father's words carefully.

"Your gift will not be fueled with rage. It's powered by love," I groaned, running his voice over and over again through my head until it made sense. Decimus pulled me into his strong arms and I pressed my lips to his chest tentatively, fully aware that the others were watching. "Thank you for helping me see that."

"See what?" He said. "Later," I whispered.

I pushed away from him at last, tipping the door open with a light shove. The others watched me with mild curiosity as I walked outside, seeing the ground covered in fresh, powdered snow. It was not meant to snow out here when it was not the dead of winter, but it looked like something else had come over the region.

My bare feet stalked through the snow and a crowd of rebels formed. I knew they were looking to me for answers, for some form of leadership that I had been unwilling to accept in the past. I couldn't let that continue.

With Decimus by my side now, I knew I'd tipped the scale of the vision.

I might have just changed the course of this war forever.

My fingertips sank into the snow as I bent forward,

inhaling slowly. I didn't think about anger, about the pains that had inflicted me in the past and in the present. I just focused on that moment in the cave when someone saw me for the first time in forever. Really saw me.

I wasn't the Head Advisor's mistake. I wasn't the highness everyone gawked at.

I was Ophelia Marshal, and I could be myself; anger and all.

My hands flicked up, and I felt the Earth move, the ground trembling as giant spikes of ice pulled out of the surface and shot into the sky like crystal towers. They lined the camp perfectly, my mind running laps on the edge of the valley, creating a frozen haven protected with cinderblocks of ice, impenetrable to everything except an atomic bomb.

I refused to let Jull defeat me with too much ease. He was going to have to work for it, just like I would work to ruin his chances of winning this war.

Besides that, I swallowed the pain of my past and thought about my parents. They gave up everything they had and more, knowing that I would take Isla back as a hero. They knew there wasn't any other way to let me acquire my birth right.

They knew the truth and let fate play out. It was time for me to stand up and accept my destiny.

The sun shined overhead, almost obscured by the towers of ice. I left the space open for the sun and for the fresh air, but this war was going to have to be fought in house. The ice was just thick enough and cloudy enough to erase any view inside or outside the new walls.

Let's just see if Jull could do this with his power.

"This is—" Terron sighed, shaking his head. He rested a heavy hand on my shoulder and gawked at the masterpiece of a wall. "You're amazing, Ophelia."

"Thank you," I breathed, turning quick so I could snatch

him up in a tight embrace. He hugged me back, refusing to release me. "Thank you for everything, Terron. You've kept me safe at my father's request for so long that it's not even a job anymore. You're family."

"You are the best little sister ever," he teased lightly, truth swirling through his tone.

"So, Ice Princess," Decimus said, resting his hand against my lower back when I let Terron go. "What's the plan?"

"First things first," I declared. "I want that combatant released from his cell."

Caspian gave me a worrisome look. "There are guns all over this camp, Ophelia. We can't let him go. There's nowhere for him to go."

"He's not going anywhere. He's going to help us."

Sig shook his head. "I don't think that's wise right now."

"I'm the Head Advisor," I snapped, my voice bouncing off the cold, crystal walls around the camp. "I say we release him."

Terron gave a firm nod, brushing past everyone while he returned to the tight jail. The combatant raced out of the hut, running for the trees that were no longer there. He paused, staring up at the frozen walls in awe.

He found my eyes next. "Why did you do this?" he groaned. "I don't want to die, please."

The man fell to his knees and bowed towards me. I shook my head at the sight, knowing what it was like to stare death in the face and just wanting to give up. I couldn't let anyone, not even my enemy's men, ever give up again.

"It's okay," I said confidently. "You're not going to die. You're going to help us."

His brows knit. "Help you? How?"

"You're the only one that knows his plans for attack. Jull's son doesn't even know what his main attack plan is after the ambush that happened a few days ago. I need you to fill in the blanks."

"I don't know anything," he vowed, nearly panting. "I was captured so long ago that he could have changed his plans. I didn't even know there was an ambush. I promise."

"I believe you. But you'll still need to show us around the capitol of Isla. It's going to be your job to get us in there unnoticed. We're going to use the portal and take the fight to him."

"Can we trust this guy?" Sig mumbled from behind me.

"I don't think we should," Matteo chimed in.

Decimus came to my side, looking at the kneeling hunter with a bit of hatred. "Hey, Smith. It's been a while."

The man looked up in shock. "Decimus. I see you're playing friendly with the enemy. Your father said he handled you after the bomb you unleashed."

"Not handled," he corrected. "Just lost track of."

Smith rose to his feet and looked at all of us carefully. His eyes landed on me next and he struggled to inhale fully, his breath hitching. "What do you need me to do?"

"You're going to go through the portal first. We will send the squads of our rebels in one by one, each group led by a different advisor. I will go with the first group."

"No, you won't," Terron snarled.

"Yeah, I second that," Caspian snapped.

"You can't go in there first," Matteo added. "It's not safe."

"It's my responsibility," I said simply. "I'm going first."

My voice carried past them all. Decimus held me tighter at my raised command. He gave me a sure nod and didn't try to correct me, didn't try to shield me. He had always known I could lead when I didn't even have the guts to think it possible. His words had been harsh in delivery, but they woke me up.

I was not a pawn anymore. I was front and center, and ready to fight.

"Everyone needs to split up into groups," I said, overlooking the crowd of rebels and the other advisors. "Work with the leader of your squad and get ready to attack. Terron, I need you to map out which group goes where. You'll have to work out a strategy for what team meets with Jull first. I want the rest of the teams to take out the other hunters.

Sig, can you make sure the portal is up and working for us? We're going to need to overwhelm it with entry and I don't need it breaking on us in the middle of this plan. Matteo, find the strongest rebels and take them with you. You're going to make sure no one leaves the capitol in this attack. I don't want the people of Isla to face retribution."

Caspian stepped forward timidly. "What do you want from me, highness?"

I smiled softly and replied, "You're going to give us our odds, Caspian. Go sit down for a while and see if you can induce a vision. I want to know how this all ends now that my mind is made up."

He nodded and everyone broke into their factions. The hunters worked with Sig to check the portal, considering he would enter it first. Decimus stayed by my side while the preparations began.

"Looks like we have a leader after all," he hummed, holding me tight. "I hope you know I'm coming with you. I have payback to avenge on my dear father."

I pulled his face down to mine for a quick kiss.

"You won't be killing Jull, Decimus. It's not your destiny."

ODDS

I sat back against the log near the bonfire, twirling my hands over in my lap. The ice that formed above my fingertips ebbed and flowed over my knuckles, moving at my will. If I remained calm, I stayed in control. It was when I was too angry to be talked down that my gift took over for good.

Leaning forward, I pressed my hands onto the rocks that lined the warm firepit. I aimed to have the ice circle the fire before smothering it, but I might be too calm for that. Even the pillars of ice around the camp were built through an influx of emotion. I just wanted us to be safe and prepared for attack. I couldn't let us get ambushed again.

Sig meandered over to where I was sitting, plopping down on the ground beside me while I toyed with my power. He crossed his arms over his knees and watched me work, the ice pulsing and glowing along the ridges of my knuckles before it spread at the snap of my fingers.

The fire died at once, a tower of smoke the only thing left to remember it by.

"Hey, that wasn't bad," Sig breathed. "The ice wall isn't a terrible touch, either."

I shrugged, feeling the sun as it bounced through the crystals and warmed my skin. "I wish I could do that without my emotions getting in the way. When I'm angry, it covers me in bruises. When I'm hopeful, it skyrockets towers into the sky. Now that I'm here, just reserved within myself, I can't do more than choke a flame out of existence."

"That's still not bad for just getting your gift, Ophelia. You haven't had it for long so don't be too hard on yourself."

I held my thumb up, watching the light crystals shine over my cold, pale skin. "It's so dangerous but it also heals. I wish I could understand that."

"Yeah, the blood on your shirt is concerning," he mentioned, pulling at the hem of my top to expose the stain he was referring to. "I would be careful about that. Jull used his powers to kill and torture. You have a chance to use it to do good."

"How is that possible when he has to die?" I asked. "I know what needs to be done, but is it something I can do? Can I kill someone?"

"He's a monster. You wouldn't be killing an innocent, that's for sure."

I stared at the smoke funnel coming from the unlit firepit. "Yeah, I get that. Terron has taken out hunters before and with no problem. But what if I choke? What if my gift attacks me instead, and I die at my own hands? I feel like I'm in over my head again, Sig."

"You were so confident earlier. What happened?"

I shook my head and sulked. "A lifetime of having no one believe in me."

"I believe in you," he reassured me. "I know we've been a little dismissive of your ideas in the past, but you stepped up.

That's how it should be. You will be the Head Advisor and we're all ready to be at that table with you."

I turned over my hand, watching my gift take over in swirly patterns around my fingers. "My father said he saw it. When I was little, he said they had to die for me to take over one day. If my parents saw what was coming, why didn't they just stop it? Why put me through this test if they weren't sure that I could succeed?"

"We all know you can succeed. You're the only one unsure of that."

I rolled my eyes. "Up until a few hours ago, you still saw me as a thorn in your side. Now I'm successful? Story of my life."

I thought about the flip that Isla had made with me. I was the rejected mistake for most of my life. They were chanting for my death! Now, once everyone had gotten sick of Jull's rule, they cheered for me to lead them. It seemed like I was constantly underestimated by everyone around me.

I'd like to say Sig and the others were different, but they really weren't. Decimus made it clear that I was just a symbol for them. He was correct. But I needed to be strong. I had to prove myself worthy of leading in this war. But I was still scared.

I would lead that first group through the portal because I promised everyone I would.

It was the staying alive that I was not certain of.

"Can I tell you something?" Sig whispered. "I just need to get it off my chest."

I nodded vehemently, needing the distraction. "Always, Sig. What's up?"

"I know I was a bully to you as a kid, and I probably should have gotten my ass kicked once or twice, but I did that because deep down, I was jealous of you."

My brows pinched. "How is that possible?"

"You were the unique one. Everyone else was a son to an advisor. You got all the attention all the time, and it wasn't until I was older that I realized it was bad attention. I didn't even consider that I was making things worse for you, either."

"It's fine, Sig. That was forever ago."

He shook his head in rebuttal. "No, it wasn't. I've been doing something worse here. All this time I promised you to lead as the Head Advisor, I've been stifling you from actually making any choices of value. I didn't want you to get too involved because I was scared you would draw focus from the goal."

I toyed with my ice, rolling it between my palms to keep myself distracted from letting it cover me again. I didn't need more bruises and cuts from my own power.

"You mean so much to Isla, Ophelia. You deserve to make decisions as you see fit. If you're going in there first, then I support you. But I think everyone here would prefer if you went in last." He cleared his throat, motioning briefly towards Decimus. "Especially hot head."

"Easy," I teased. "He's not a bad guy."

"You know he tried to kill me, right?"

I cringed slightly, wondering how much they got past their previous encounter while I was knocked out in jail. "Yeah, but that's history, right?"

He shrugged. "I guess if you say it is."

"It is," I reaffirmed. "Jull has divided our realm enough. We don't need to help him."

He smiled gently, his hand resting on my knee, but I could see his reservations still stood. I'd gotten rather close to Sig through this whole ordeal. Having him upset like this only made my heart ache more. I rested my hand on top of his, trying to soothe him, but I was not very good at doing that for myself let alone anyone else.

"So, what do you think of him?"

I sat up straighter at his vague question. "What are you talking about?"

We both flicked a look at Decimus who was talking with Smith. I could see them working together on a map through the capital. Decimus wasn't successful with his bombing attempt before, but he knew enough about the capital after that trial and error to help lead the way through it.

He met my eyes briefly, grinning from across the camp before going back to his diligent work. He wanted revenge against his father, that scar on his neck beckoning for vengeance. If anyone deserved to get revenge against Jull, it was him. That dictator tried to kill his own son and had killed Decimus' mother, forcing Decimus into hiding ever since.

Thinking about how long he had spent alone, I knew I wouldn't have made it. Terron got me through the worst of moments, but he wouldn't have to do that after today. The sun was going down in Wyoming. It was in sync with Isla so I knew the night would be there soon. We needed to catch Jull off-guard, at the end of his day. And that time was almost upon us.

I left Sig with a smile, walking towards Caspian who was tucked into the furthest spot possible in the camp, his back to the ice barrier. He was in a meditative pose on the ground, legs crossed with his eyes closed. His hands rested evenly over each knee, his methodical breathing so relaxed that it made me yawn.

He poked one eye open and bowed his head in respect. "Highness. Have a seat."

I sat beside him, overlooking the camp and the training rebels from afar. Matteo had picked the biggest of the bunch. They were looking over their guns and practicing hand-to-hand combat. I wished I was strong enough to participate in something like that, but I'd be going in empty-handed.

Hopefully, my gift would be enough.

"So, any word from the future?" I breathed.

He leaned back, stretching his legs out straight. "Yeah, I got a couple of glimpses."

"What are the odds we win this?"

"Fifty percent for now," he mumbled. "But there's something concerning we need to talk about first, highness."

"Okay, what's wrong now?"

He rotated his thumbs over one another while staring off into the distance. "I could be wrong, because that happens, you know? The betrayal scene I showed you has obviously changed because you stepped in and flipped course."

"Yeah, so what? What did you see now?"

He paused longer this time. "It's complicated, really. I didn't get a great look—"

"Tell me now, Caspian."

He finally surrendered. "In every vision I've had so far, you don't make it."

"What?" I breathed. "I don't make it inside the portal or make it to the capital? What are you saying, Caspian?"

His face darkened while he steadied his breath long enough to swallow the budding lump in his throat. I'm starting to feel one in mine, too. I held back the ice from overtaking me again, forcing my emotions to settle for now.

"You die at the end of all my visions."

I leaned back, the urge to unleash my emotions even more daunting than before. Still, I relaxed, tapping the tips of my fingers together one by one. He'd been on point with some of his visions, while others had been a little off. If I was able to change the direction of fate, then I could change the outcome of what he saw for me.

But what if it was truly just fate?

"Tell me something, Caspian."

"Of course, highness. Anything."

"Does Jull die in the end of those as well?"

"Only half of them. We either defeat his whole army and take him down at the end, or he escapes out the back door and we only manage to take down the hunters and combatants."

I shook my head in mild confusion. "So, how am I meant to die if he escapes?"

"I just see ice. It covers your throat, your whole body, and eats at your lungs, down to your heart. I don't know if it's because of you or Jull, but I know it's what happens no matter what. I don't know how to prevent this one for you."

"Yeah, there's no avoiding my ice," I admitted. This wasn't something I could just make go away with a shift of fate. It was up to me and Jull. It was up to the circumstances of war and sometimes war was just unforgiving. "One more thing," I sighed. "You can't tell anyone else about this."

He groaned under his breath. "Highness, please. You need to be open with the others. We are your advisors in Isla. We're on your team."

"Exactly why no one can know my fate," I repeated. "Just keep it to yourself, please."

He finally agreed but his body went tense, the crimson of his eyes flickering bright ruby while he sat up straighter. "Another problem," he muttered. "My brother is back."

TRICKS

$\mathcal{I}$ pressed my hands into the ice wall, careful not to send the pillars crashing down as I did so. I managed to shove a block back, spying a weird, wounded figure in the distance. Caspian held on my arm to keep me from approaching. The other advisors hurried to my side, all of us carefully watching the limping figure in the woods.

"What is that?" Matteo gusted.

"Not what, but who," Caspian replied. "It's my brother."

"The traitor," Terron said, his jaw locked. "Elson should be left out of here. You should patch up the wall and we can move on to our training."

I waved off his suggestion almost immediately. "Do what you want, but I want to talk to him."

"We're in the middle of war preparation, Ice Princess." Decimus rested his hand on my shoulder and looked toward the setting sun behind Elson, whose body was stooped forward while his clothes were streaked with blood. "He gave up on you too soon. You can't take him back now."

"Sure, I can," I muttered. "He's obviously in no shape to double-cross us again. Besides, I'm curious what happened.

He couldn't have made that choice easily. What if he has a good reason for running to Jull other than just some off-chance of a vision where I betrayed everyone?"

"It's not really like that," Caspian groaned. "My visions come true more than you think, highness. That's why you should be careful."

I shot him a narrow look and he gave up, staring at the grass. We all waited patiently for Elson to come within a close enough distance before Sig called for him to stop. When he halted, he fell to his knees, his clothes and skin stained with vermillion cuts.

"What happened to you?" I asked, speaking loud enough for him to catch my words from afar. "Is this another ploy of some kind?"

"I didn't want to double cross anyone," he called back, "I just had to see for myself what happened."

"What are you talking about?" I probed carefully, treading in the middle of the advisors, and the wounded outcast. "What did you see?"

He glanced up, his eyes bruised in the center. "I left camp one night after I saw the vision my brother had about your betrayal."

"You ran to Jull and got us all attacked!" Terron bit.

Elson shook his head. "No, that's not right. I ran into some combatants while I was out. I managed to escape but I was too embarrassed to tell everyone what happened, so I dropped it. I didn't even see Jull, so I figured it was nothing. I didn't know he would have hunters follow me back to camp. When they attacked, they took me with them."

I cocked my head to the side, lost in his words. "Why did you leave camp in the first place? What did you see from Caspian's vision concerning my betrayal?"

"That's just it, highness. I didn't see your betrayal."

I took another step closer, feeling the guys behind me

grow more tense with every step. "Okay, so walk me through what you saw."

"It's not good," he warned.

"That's fine. I need to know."

It couldn't be the worst thing I'd heard today, that was for sure.

I sank to my knees before him, the marks on his face too devastating to miss. He bowed his head with me being this close, proving his loyalty was still with my legacy.

"I saw you as a child," he whispered, eyes cast down. "You couldn't have been older than a toddler. Your mother was gone, but your father was still alive. Jull came into the room and held out his hand for you. There was a snowflake on it."

I stirred at the memory. "I know what you're talking about. I remember that day. He got into an argument outside with the other advisors."

"Do you recall what that fight consisted of?"

"I don't know, actually. It was the last time I saw Jull before he came back to kill everyone at the capitol."

He nodded at my recollection, but I knew I was missing something. "He was arguing about you, Ophelia. The others were talking about killing you, but he stuck up for you and your father. He didn't want you to die."

"That's ironic," I groaned. "He seems pretty keen on killing me now."

"It didn't make any sense to me, either. I had to meditate to have it make sense, but that's when everything went wrong, and I ran into the hunters."

"All right, I believe you," I said without hesitation. "Caspian, come help your brother back into camp and I'll see if I can heal him."

The red-eyed brother hesitated. "Highness, are you—"

"Just do it," I snapped. "I trust him."

Caspian obliged and even Terron helped, picking Elson

up and dragging him back through the ice wall. I held my breath and pushed the block back into place, feeling the ice tether back into the pillars instantly.

"What's the plan now?" Decimus whispered against my ear, his lips brushing my cheek. "You're cold, Ophelia. You need to warm up."

I shook my head, my hands trembling at my sides. "I don't think that's possible."

I watched Caspian walk his brother across camp and head for their cabin. I knew I needed to heal Elson soon, but we had the attack to worry about. I swallowed hard and looked to Decimus's sweet, calm grin.

He deserved to know the truth about the vision my friend kept seeing. If it was going to end up being my fate, no matter what I tried, then I should be open about it.

But I wouldn't ruin that perfect grin or those mirthful blue eyes for anything. Instead, I caught my breath and rolled my cold palms against my shirt, knowing that the time was near for us to attack. I stood on the tips of my toes and dusted my lips against his.

His hand slid into my hair and I wanted to dissolve beneath his fingertips, the warmth of his body so enticing. "Everything okay?" he asked. "You're quiet. That makes me feel like something is wrong."

I shook my head. "No, nothing is wrong. I'm going to go heal Elson and then we should get a move on to Isla. It's time to take down your father."

His knuckle dragged down my neck. "We need to get your necklace back, too."

I reached for the spot on my throat that was left bare, missing the moonstone more than anything else. Decimus kissed my forehead and then returned to the rebels, prepping for war. I watched him go and then I wound through the crowd to get to Elson's cabin where Terron and Caspian were waiting on the doorstep. Terron stopped me first, his hand light on my bruised arm.

"He doesn't want you to heal him," Terron said, shaking his head. "He said he doesn't deserve your forgiveness."

"He's right," Caspian sighed.

I ignored them both, pushing into the cabin to see Elson lying in bed. The ice on my fingertips started to grow at the sight of his wounds. I had my own to deal with, as well. Still, Elson sat up in bed, holding his hand out to stop me.

"No, please, highness. I don't want your help. I don't deserve your mercy."

"Too bad," I muttered. "I am going to help you. Everyone deserves forgiveness."

He didn't stop me again while I scattered ice over his surface, spreading it casually across his body without relent. He trembled at the cold temperature, the ice lacing his face and his arms, healing every mark slowly before water dripped from his skin afterwards.

I staggered upright, feeling rather weak from such a simple task. I tried not to let it show, making my way to the door, when his gentle tone stopped me.

"Are you going to kill Jull?"

I swallowed the lump in my throat and shrugged. "I'm not sure yet. Why?"

"Because I don't think he wants to kill you."

I waved off that thought entirely. "He definitely wants to kill me. I'm the reason there are rioters in the first place. Without me, there's no uprising. He wants me dead to end it."

"Did he say that?"

I pondered his simple question for a long minute. In some way, he was right. Jull never did say he would kill me. He'd mentioned that he couldn't kill me at the carnival. Earlier than that, he had his hunters shoot a dart at me, but that was so I could be dragged off without a fight. I couldn't be positive if he would have killed me or not.

But he did try to kill his own son before.

Why wouldn't he want me dead, too?

"I have to do something, Elson. I can't just sit around and wait for him to kill me. He's tortured the people of Isla for a long time. It's pointless to spare him. He's too powerful to subdue. He's used his ice to do too much harm in the realm. We have to kill him."

He hung his head in response. "All right, if you say the word, then it'll be done highness."

"Are you going into the portal with us?"

He chewed on his lips in a nervous trance. "No, I don't think I should. I'll stay back. My gift is of no use in this battle."

I gave him the benefit of being right and left on that note. Caspian caught my hand when I walked away, pulling me toward him. His eyes were the deepest shade of red I'd ever seen before. The deep maroon color made my soul ache.

"I don't want you to go in there," he gusted, staring worriedly at the portal. "Your odds are nothing, Ophelia. Whether you live or die, that's the most important thing here."

"No, it's about what I do with Jull," I corrected him. "I need to try at least to get our realm back. It's our home, Caspian. Don't you want your home realm back? You can take your father's position, you and Elson both."

He gripped my wrist a little tighter. "Not like this."

"I have to do what's right," I repeated, tired of defending my actions. "I will just give it my best shot and go from there. I've been on borrowed time, anyway. Everyone has been saying I should die for decades. If it's my fate, then it's my fate."

He pulled me against his side and nodded. Moonlight

shined over me, filling the gap in the ice wall. I made my way towards the portal, the sores and cuts on my body still throbbing. I needed to heal myself but I couldn't, too afraid it would get out of hand like it had in the past. There was no reason to add more wounds to the mix.

Everyone gathered with guns in hands, the advisors ready to trudge through the portal. I looked at them all thoughtfully, our little group of rebels attempting to take down the biggest dictator in all of the realms.

All I could ask for was an easy fix to my massive problem.

"I know we're not as big as Jull's army," I said, my voice faking confidence. "We're not the most equipped to start this war in the first place. I just turned nineteen a few weeks ago. I didn't think this would be the result. But everyone here has ties to Isla. Whether it's family to protect, or titles to reclaim, we have to get back what's rightfully ours."

Everyone thrummed, cheering at my words. I let them bask in this positive moment just in case it was the last we ever got. Still, I had to adhere to the goal in mind, my blood running cold at the thought. I looked for Decimus, finding Terron first as he came onto the platform, taking me in his arms.

We may have had a rocky relationship these last few years, but he would always be my older brother. He couldn't protect me anymore, and I thought he realized that, holding me tighter and longer than normal.

"It's going to be okay," I panted, nodding slowly.

Caspian shook his head, watching us. He tucked his eyes to the ground instead of towards me. I wanted to run up and hug him tight too, but he left to be with his brother for now, the two of them needing to stay out of the final fight. I didn't want anyone getting hurt that couldn't properly defend themselves—aside from me, who still needed to learn a thing or two about defending herself. I just didn't have the luxury of staying behind. I needed to be there with my team, with the other rebels, and we had to take back what was ours.

My father died for Isla. If it was my destiny to do the same, it would be an honor.

"Hey, Ice Princess," Decimus sighed, coming towards me when Terron finally let go. I gave him a hopeful look before being scooped up into Decimus' arms. "You're going to do great, Ophelia. I'll be in the team right behind you."

I nodded, riding on that promise. "Just be careful, please," I whispered, hugging him tight.

"I should be telling you to do that," he breathed. "It's going to work out. I know it will. You can handle your own, you even took me down a notch."

"I'll do it again if you get hurt out there," I warned with a smile.

He set me down, his lips finding mine. When we pulled away, our eyes remained locked for a long time before I finally took a step back.

I caught Sig in passing, our favorite techy working hard at getting the portal ready to use as a door, not just a window. I caught him in the middle of his haste, his eyes downcast and saddened.

"What's wrong?" I probed, hoping that he was okay.

He shook his head, flicking a look towards Decimus briefly. "It's nothing, Ophelia. I'm just really happy for you."

"Happy for me?" I gusted. "Is that possible? We're about to go to intergalactic war with a murderous, frosty dictator who hates my guts. I'd say I don't have a lot for someone to be happy for me."

"You've just come a long way. Even found someone you care for. It's nice to see," he added, though there was still a twinge of sadness in his tone. "I've got this thing ready to go. The call is on you now, highness."

I blushed, looking for Matteo. I waved him over from his

group of strong men. "Are you ready? I'm going to need you and your group to man the exits and entrances. If they're outside, keep them out. If they're inside—"

"Destroy them," he rattled with a proud grin. "I'm ready, Ophelia. Let's get this done."

I looked to the buzzing crowd. My nerves were shot. "Whoever is coming with me, we're going in first," I hummed as Smith stepped up to join me and my team. "Are you ready?" I asked him. "I don't know the place very well. Just some vague memories."

"I'll get you where you need to be," he replied dutifully.

"Then I guess we're ready to go."

Sig turned on the portal, a low and thrumming buzz coming over the hushed crowd.

For a moment, everything was calm and silent. I wished it could stay like this forever.

FIND HIM

Smith walked in first, a group of five to six rebels following him close by. I held my breath, reaching through the swirl of color and light that was the portal. I gave Decimus one last look over my shoulder and then I touched the realm briefly with my fingertips, unable to contain my nerves much longer.

I was finally going home.

I stepped inside, feeling a wash of cold air swarm past me like a wave pool. I stammered to keep upright. It was a daunting task, jumping through millions of lightyears of realms in only one step.

It was like being kicked in the gut with a metal boot. I still hadn't healed myself, still stuck with blood and cuts that lined my body from earlier. My gift was on edge, forming over my hands while I took in the foyer of the capitol.

The last time I was here, I was practically a toddler. My father died in the boardroom, Jull laid waste to everyone in his way, and the world seemed to stop turning. Standing on the marble floors, I felt everything and more now, overlooking the white columns that shot off into the roof with delicate, ornate gold details encrusting the walls and doors.

I took my first breath of Isla for the first time in forever. It filled my lungs and sated my homesick tick. Glancing around, Smith pointed to a hallway nearby. Hunters lined every other door, including the ones that made up the front of the capitol.

"It's oddly quiet for a place in the middle of a war," I mumbled.

Smith shook his head. "I have a bad feeling about this."

I straightened my posture, hoping to get a good sense about this endeavor, but Caspian's warning still loomed through my mind. I didn't wake up meaning to die, but I'd do it if necessary. I just didn't want anyone else to get caught in the middle of it.

Thankfully, Matteo and his team came through next. I pointed them towards the entrance of the capitol while urging my group down the hall. My makeshift plan better work or else we were in more trouble than I could imagine.

Steadying my breath, I fired off a wave of ice through the building, watching it come crashing down on men in all-black uniforms. I peered around the corner to judge my good work, or to get shot down so fast—I couldn't be certain. Smith and I took the leap, peering down the hall to see Jull's men all frozen to the floor.

Their eyes were moving, but I was certain they would suffocate if I left them like this. One of the hunters noticed my apprehension and Smith looked at each of them carefully, pointing at the scrawny soldier in the back.

"This is Hue," he sighed. "He is Jull's assistant. He will know what's going on and where to find Jull. Maybe he can tell us why it's so quiet in here, as well. Something isn't right."

I brought my hands over his frame just in time to hear

heavy steps coming down the hallway behind us. I turned to see Decimus leading his men through the soldier-popsicles. He smiled as he brought his lips to mine, even if we were just together moments ago.

"Look at what you've done," Decimus joked. "Only been here three minutes and you've already created an ice box in the capitol."

"Hopefully it doesn't need to get much worse than this," I groaned. "Think you can thaw this one out for me? I have yet to master unfreezing things."

"Of course." He brushed the ice with his glowing, orange fingertips, flames licking through the ice until we could poke a hole through the structure of it. Decimus ripped the cracked blocks apart and ice scattered along the floor in a loud crash. "There we go. All warm now."

The soldier was panting to catch his breath, shivering while ice tainted his eyelashes. "Thank you for sparing me, highness."

My brows pinched. "What did you just call me?"

He bowed his head, surrendering on his hands and knees while bowing down almost obnoxiously. "Highness. You're the rightful ruler of Isla."

I gave Decimus a panicked look. Sig found us moments later while he ran through the empty foyer. The three of us pondered the young man's words for a moment and I nudged Decimus to undo the ice on the other combatants.

Sig kicked their guns aside but they hardly seemed concerned over them, each one climbing to a panting, struggling stance before me.

"What is going on here?" I groaned, watching them all bow outright. "Someone explain what is happening right now."

"Highness," Hue groaned. "Jull has our families in his barracks. We didn't want to fight in this war, but he said he'd have them all killed if one of us didn't agree to fight. We stand with you, Ophelia. Just please, find our families."

I swallowed hard, looking to Decimus.

"So, I have to defeat Jull, save Isla as a realm, and free all of his hostages?" I muttered. "What am I supposed to do?"

"You can do this," he whispered. "I'll lead my team through the capitol and to the barracks. I've been there before but escaped. I can get them out the back doors to refrain from getting caught in this fight."

"You have to be careful," Hue pointed out. "There are still some men that are on his side. They'll catch you the first chance they get, highness."

"Catch or kill?" I questioned.

The false hunters all exchanged a weary look.

"I'm not sure, actually," Hue shrugged his shoulders and sat up on his knees, "he told us to kill everyone but you. Jull wants you alive, highness."

"I knew it. He's wants to do it himself. Make an example out of me," I groaned.

Sig chimed in, his eyes flicking to the lights. "I say we shut this place down. They have the upper hand with lights and cameras on. They might be hearing this all as we speak."

The doors across the foyer burst open and Matteo rushed over, breathless. "Ophelia, you have to come see this."

I pushed past everyone, hearing their steps all follow in sync. Matteo parted the door open, exposing the streets of Isla. It was just like I recalled. Pointed roofs, marble streets, and curbs of gold, the buildings were crafted in stunning white rock with silver veins tracing through them.

Aside from the nostalgia, there was nothing else for me to see.

"Everything is empty," Matteo whispered. "The store-fronts, the homes. We ventured out a few blocks and found nothing. What should we do now?"

I shook my head, unsure what to say. "We need to find Jull but—the residents are being kept in the barracks, but there's no way he has them all," I panted. My heart was racing too fast. "We—we should—"

Decimus drew his hand around my hip, his body pulsing in heat. "It's okay. Calm down. Trust yourself. Just think about the options."

I gave him a helpless look. Everyone was focused on me, waiting for a reply, waiting to be told where we were going. My sides were sewn with ice and I shuddered, fighting to keep down the panic as it bubbled through me.

"I don't know," I whispered.

A spray of gunfire stole everyone's focus, the sound peppering the walls inside. Decimus pushed me to the ground, the rebels with guns pointing towards the doors while we waited to see what happened. I trembled in angst, unsure who they were firing at.

Everyone came in already, right?

I looked around, studying each advisor carefully, knowing I was missing someone. The brothers were on Earth, but someone else was just ambushed in the foyer. My heart leaped out of my chest when I realized who it was.

I shoved past Decimus, breaking through the door, finding a familiar man stooped over on the ground. Terron clung to his hip, blood seeping through his fingers while he groaned from the pain.

A stray bullet hit the wall nearby. I looked at our rebels, all wounded, dying, or dead from the sudden attack. Decimus sent his group ahead to follow the sounds of retreat as I delicately pushed my hands into Terron's side. I could see him struggling to stay awake, to stay alive, but his cool eyes drifted over me all the same.

"You need to get out of here," he pleaded, shaking his head. "I need you to go, Ophelia."

"I'm not leaving. I can fix you," I panted.

Somehow through the heat of the moment, I could think clearly. "Decimus, go to the barracks. Take Matteo with you and some rebels. You need to get those prisoners out of there. Hue, go with Sig. I need you all to cut the power so Jull doesn't see me coming.

Terron's brow furrowed. "You're not going alone."

"Of course not," I sighed. "I'm going to heal you and we will go there together. Got it?"

He reluctantly nodded as everyone parted at once. This was no time for sappy goodbyes and careful warnings. I tended to Terron as best as possible, spreading ice over his waist while he inhaled deeply, groaning as the bullet hole vanished. I did the same to his lower back that sported the exit wound.

Smith knelt, pushing his finger to his lips while an odd creaking sound came over the capitol. "Power is about to be cut. Do you have a flashlight?"

"There's one on the rifles," Terron said, breaking it off and tossing it over to me. He stood, still sore, leaning sideways while he caught his balance. His fingertips poked at the cold spot that once sported a bullet hole. "That's pretty helpful. The guns are empty, though. We're out of ammunition already."

"Could be worse."

The power cuts off suddenly, leaving everyone in the dark.

I inhaled calmly at last. "Looks like we're even now."

OUR GIFT

erron led the way purely out of stubbornness. He poked his head around the corner of each intersection, searching for the next venture to take. Smith was pretty smart with his directional skills, leading us through the hallways without fail.

Heavy steps rang out through the hallway and Terron smothered his light, shoving me into the wall while it felt like someone ran right past us in the pitch dark. I swallowed the lump in my throat, the fear of getting shot becoming more and more overwhelming.

I held Terron's hand for comfort, letting him lead the way under Smith's whispering voice. We came to the end of the narrow hall and the walls opened up with a glint of moonlight shining through the windows overhead. The space was grand but empty, something so eerie about the circular dome of a room.

Terron tucked the light into his pocket, the two of us stalking towards the hallway nearby to check it out, but a single shot rang out. Smith hit the floor, gargling on his own blood while I shoved Terron behind me. He tried to protest, hardwired to protect me, but even as a strategist he should have known this was the safest move.

They wouldn't kill me, so I stood front and center to prevent the same for Terron.

A rival soldier lowered his rifle from across the room, sidestepping out of the way for the main event himself. Jull emerged. He was thinner than I last saw him in the seer's vision. He was so lean but sunken in around the eyes. His fingers were boney while they sat on the edge of a tall, narrow staff. Something was frozen in his dead, gray eyes.

"Hey, sweetheart. Long time, no see," he purred.

I winced, seeing my necklace strung across his throat in a bold taunt. "Give that back to me."

"What?" he gusted, stroking the moonstone obviously. "You want this back? Why would you think you'd need this, Ophelia? It's a silly old necklace your mother probably stole off of someone while she was still alive."

"Don't talk about my mother," I barked.

"Your poor, sick mother," he said with a hint of sarcasm in his tone. "She should have never stolen this necklace in the first place."

"She didn't steal it!"

Smith choked slightly, spitting up blood while his body gave way. Terron kept me perfectly still, clutching his hand into my hip to keep me from moving. I knew we should have found a gun with a bullet or two left, but I always knew this would come down to a battle of our gifts.

I swallowed hard and lunged for Smith, my hands pressing into his neck where he had already bled out most of his body on the marble floors. Terron ducked beside me, helping Smith keep conscious while the wounds in his throat slowly tethered back together.

"Okay," I panted, wiping the blood onto my pants.

Jull hadn't moved, leaning on his staff while he was

surrounded by combatants in black masks. "That was brave of you, sweetheart." He flicked a look to his hunters. "Kill the traitor and the other advisor kid. Now."

The guns raised and I shoved them both back, panting in panic while I used myself as a shield. Terron held onto me carefully while Smith whispered for mercy under his breath.

"Don't hurt them," I pleaded. "They don't have to die. Just me."

"No," Terron snarled. "You won't give yourself up."

"I will if it saves everyone."

Jull stood taller, a sly smile on his lips. "You think I want you dead, sweetheart?"

I nodded profusely. "Why else have you done all of this? You started a war on Earth, you chased me and Terron down. You've done nothing but torment my mind and the minds of my seers! You're a monster."

"I may be a monster," he grumbled, "but get one thing clear. I never wanted you dead. You strictly had to be kept alive to be of use to me."

My brows furrowed. "Of use to you how? Why do you want me this bad? To start a bloodbath of a battle?"

"You have your seers, your parents had theirs—I had one of my own, sweetheart. He told me that you would be the key to unlocking my powers fully. Without you, I will always be second tier. I need to achieve the very best level now. I need you for that."

"I can't help you with that," I gusted. "I—I hardly know how to use this power."

"I have everything set up already, Ophelia. Don't worry. If you surrender now, I'll let everyone go. Including your little friends that I caught in the security room."

My heart flipped in my chest. If I had anything to throw, I would. "You have Sig?"

He nodded slowly. "Yeah. Soon I'll have the rest of them, too. Even the ones on Earth."

"You can't! I built a wall to protect them!"

He smiled coyly, shaking his head. "You're so cute, Ophelia. You built a wall to keep me out of the woods. But you just opened the door to the portal, and last I checked, there's still a way to go through and come back without trouble."

My eyes softened in agony. "Oh no…"

"I'll have every single advisor lined up one by one unless you come with me. We can just start picking them off the line, starting with your favorite bodyguard here."

Jull ripped the pistol from another hunter and aimed it at Terron's face. I choked at the sight of his brutality, daring to kill a man that was more like my brother than any sibling ever could be. I stepped forward, letting that angst overwhelm me.

Ice sparked up from my stance, forming crystal daggers that grew in height until they reached the base of Jull's shoes, the tip of the ice poking into his chin. I watched him step back a little bit, removing the ice spikes from his neck.

A tiny trail of blood swirled down his neck and I grinned at the sight.

I might not be the best at this gift, but making Jull bleed from it proved that I was going to be all right. I swallowed the lump in my throat, and he tucked the pistol into his back waistband. He took the moment to nod at my actions, seeing the wall of spikes that I just created from the marble floors.

"You've been practicing," he hummed.

I shook my head. "Hardly. But if I can do that without practice, imagine what I can create when you push me even further."

He held onto his staff, clearing his throat so the hunters flanking him lowered their weapons at last. I went stiff at their abrupt movements, seeing them disappear into the dark corridors, leaving him alone.

His gaze turned to Smith and Terron. I pleaded that they abide for once and leave. Terron refused at first, but I begged with my misty eyes that he go. He needed to save himself, save the innocent of Isla, and I couldn't do that with him breathing down my neck as my protector.

It was time I protected him, after all.

When it was just Jull and me, my heart slowed. Just having me calm down was enough to settle the ice wall I had just created in the middle of the dome. It melted to nothing, puddling at our feet. He kicked the water with amusement.

"That was a fun party trick, sweetheart. What else can you do?"

I shook my head. "I don't want to talk about that. I want to know why you've come after me. You had the realm all to yourself. Why come for me over the whim of some seer?"

"Because that vision was very important to me," he retorted. "I saw colorful lights exuding through ice that came from your fingertips. I didn't know it was ice back then, but it makes sense now. It was so stunning and unknown—I have to know how it's done. I want you to be on my team, Ophelia. The people of Isla love you, after all."

"They love me because they hate you," I growled. "It's not the same."

He shrugged off my words as nothing more than a causal taunt. "Yeah, but you miss it here, don't you? Running all over those little realms of yours. Earth is a cesspool of humans, and Topree is divorcing itself from the inside out with thieves and rogues. You're not going to find somewhere more like home than Isla."

"You ruined what used to be my home," I growled. "You took everything away from me, and more! If you think that

I'm going to let that happen again, then you're wrong. Isla is my home, not yours."

He shook his head, twirling his cane in his hands. "That's a shame, Ophelia. I didn't want to make a prisoner out of you, but I'll subdue you as long as I need until I see that power of yours really break through."

"You want to see my power?" I snapped. "Then watch!"

Ice flew through the air, except it volleyed from both directions. Jull and me. He landed a spike into my shoulder while I cut his leg, tearing his flesh like he penetrated mine. I needed a minute to heal, to collect myself, so I pulled a wall between us, pushing it from one end of the room to the other. He snickered through the block, his blurred image stalking closer.

"You don't get it, do you?"

He pushed both hands out, the wall of ice breaking suddenly and throwing large blocks toward me. He adjusted his blazer like a magician might to show how easy this was for him. He kicked the splinters of ice aside and grinned ear to ear.

"You can throw all those tricks for the others, but there is nothing I haven't already seen, sweetheart."

He charged forward, his hand outstretched and covered with ice, pushing into my neck and slamming my back into the wall. He backed up, his hand leaving my throat, but the ice remained, suffocating me while I was pinned to the wall still.

I scratched at the block of ice, fighting to make it melt, but I knew panicking wasn't going to save me. Instead, I relaxed and closed my eyes, thinking of what calmed me the most. Decimus' eyes came into my mind and water trickled off my throat until I was free.

"Very good," Jull purred. "You're getting stronger. I just

want to see that one little trick you have now. Show me the lights, Opehlia."

I shook my head, still unsure what he was talking about. I didn't even have useful tricks with my gift, let alone astonishing ones like what he was describing. I drew ice around the floor where he stood and shot it upright like a raw crystal, pinning him inside.

I waited for him to melt out of it and make his grand escape, but I could see him begin to panic inside the ice block. I could let him choke without air, or allow his body to freeze and die as it would naturally in Antarctica on Earth. I was still not that cruel, feeling a pit in my stomach at the thought of seeing someone dying by my hands.

Catching my breath, I relaxed again, letting the ice shave off of his body and fall to the floor like panes of glass.

"Dammit," he choked, coughing up water while his entire frame was covered in cold moisture. "You're really going to start pissing me off, little girl."

I shook my head, "I don't want to kill you, Jull. I just want to know *why*."

His brows furrowed and his eyes deepened in hue "Why what?" He picked himself up off the floor and leaned on his cane for support. "Why have I come after you? I told you that."

"I want to know why you stuck up for me! Why did you argue with the advisors and why did you kill them?" My voice cracked, seeing my father's sad features in my mind. "Why did you kill my father?"

He sported a small smile and finally, I saw something resembling empathy cross his face. "You want to know what caused this whole domino effect, huh?"

Cold tears brimmed my eyes. "More than anything else."

"You were the mistake, Ophelia. Everyone was voting to have you killed. Your father was against it, you were already two years old, but he knew something was wrong. He knew something would be different with you."

I stared at my palms, knowing that it was the truth. "Did he know my gift?"

He shook his head. "No, of course not. That would have fast-tracked everything, and he would have killed you sooner, I'm sure of it. But I saw something in you that caught my eyes. I wasn't going to let you die when I found out what you could do."

My eyes narrowed. "The thing with the lights?"

"Precisely," he hummed. "You don't get it, though. It wasn't some reflection of lights. It was prisms of powers coursing from your fingertips and unleashing on the realms, Ophelia! You could wield the power of the world's worst blizzard, and I don't doubt that you could rule Earth, Topree, and Isla with a flick of your wrist."

"That's what I wanted back then. Seeing that kind of power made my blood warm. Finding out a few weeks ago that your gift was ice as well—that just sweetened the deal."

I sniffled at his words, cool tears falling down my pale cheeks. "Are you saying you killed my father so you could one day try to use my powers?" I grunted. "You killed everyone so that you could use me as a *weapon*?"

He smiled proudly. "You're the only weapon in the world worth having, sweetheart. I just need you to join me. We could rule Isla together. I'll let you have the realm all to yourself, but I want that trick of yours to use as my own. I will rule Earth and Topree with it."

I clenched my hands into taut fists at my sides. "You wanted a weapon. You've got one."

CRESCENDO

I threw everything I had at that power hungry monster. I wielded daggers of ice, spat balls of snow, and laced the room with so much glassy crystal that it started to suck the air out of the room. I encased us both deeper and deeper into the room, bringing layers of ice into stacked blocks of concrete, unable to be kicked through with even the strongest of gifts.

Jull watched in awe, dodging my threats as I threw them at him relentlessly. It was easily below freezing in our little cocoon of ice, drowning out everything else while he stared at the ceiling, watching it cave in with thicker plates of clear crystal.

I took this opportunity to snatch my necklace back, my palm wrapping around the moonstone, but the chain was still hooked around his throat. He yanked me forward, clinging to my arm with a grasp that could break my hand in half if he wanted to.

I swallowed the lump in my throat and looked into his chilly eyes. "Let go of me."

"Let go of *my* necklace," he taunted. "You don't deserve

the moonstone, sweetheart. You shouldn't have ever been gifted such a stone. It's for the powerful. This here," he added, pointing to the sphere of ice that we were trapped inside of now, like a snow globe, "this is a tantrum. You better show me the real power, Ophelia. Or I have no use for you."

My hand clutched the stone of my necklace tighter. "I don't have that power. If I did, I would use it against you, anyway."

He nodded slowly. "Of course. Well, I guess that answers that."

He pulled the gun from his waistband and pressed the barrel to my chest. He didn't even flinch or give me a chance to react, pulling the trigger and letting my body fly backward in recoil from the gunshot.

The ice fell with me, water puddling on the floors and smearing my blood against the marble where I lay, useless and dying. I pressed my hand to my chest, needing to heal the mark, but I couldn't feel my power anymore.

I could hardly feel anything at all.

I stared at the ceiling and the moon outside the windows. It wouldn't be a bad last view, except the sounds of hurried steps rushed through the hall and came to a screeching halt next to me. Decimus leaned forward, his palm plugging the hole in my body, but it was useless.

I'd lost enough blood to just give up now.

He was weeping softly, his hand crawling up the side of my neck and lifting my head off the hard, wet tiles. "Hey, Ice Princess. You're going to be okay."

Jull's laughter filled the dome. "Oh, what a joke. Come on, son. Don't give her false hope at the end of her life. She needs to hear the truth now. Truth is, you will never be an advisor, Ophelia. You're no better than your rotten, pathetic father! You will accept his fate, too."

I clung to Decimus, knowing that the spots over my vision couldn't be good. "My—My mother's—necklace."

Decimus glared at his father. He left my side briefly. I heard a scuffle, but Jull didn't fight his son too much over the trinket. Decimus returned to my side, kneeling in my blood so he could draw the chain around my head and let it rest against the hollow of my throat.

I had felt naked without it.

"Hey," Decimus breathed, kissing my cheek softly. "I love you, Ophelia. You're stronger than they all think you are. Just remember that, okay?"

I wished I could reply. I tasted iron shooting up my throat while I nearly choked to death on my own blood. I couldn't imagine this was what the people of Isla wanted from me when they said they wanted me dead as a child.

Now I was letting them all down by not staying alive.

If I could change it, I would.

"Everyone is out," Decimus whispered. "They're all safe, okay? You were successful today, Ophelia. You saved everyone."

Everyone but myself.

"Let her go, son," Jull snarled. "She's had this coming for a long, long time. Let her death happen slowly, painfully, knowing that she failed her people. I still own the realm, after all! As long as I'm alive, I won't let anyone else control Isla."

Decimus balled his fists, fire tainting his skin, but I managed to brush his knee with my hand, calming him down. His focus returned to me and I watched my vision fade at his look of sadness.

Truth be told, I had fallen for Decimus too.

My chest lurched in shock. The moonstone on my neck began to burn and throb against my skin. I hissed a breath, my eyes flying open before they shut for good as Decimus backed up in horror. I released the loudest, most daunting scream I could create, the noise echoing off the walls and ringing throughout the capitol.

My necklace was burning hot to the touch, and I gasped, pushing my hands out on the floor beside me until, with a flick of my wrist, a gorgeous array of pastels smeared through the air. I swiped the air, and the colors followed as I dropped my palm onto the bullet wound on my skin.

The mark tethered with the source of light still spinning from my fingertips. I felt more alive than ever, pushing to an unsteady stance while Decimus crawled back in shock. Jull stood his ground, his eyes widened as the assortment of light exploded around my body. I felt more powerful than I ever had, practically floating while I harnessed everything I could to defeat this monster once and for all.

"What—how are you—" Jull asked, desperate to wield this power as his own.

I shook my head and replied, "It's a secret reserved for the truly powerful."

Whipping my hands out in front of me, the light tackled Jull backward, his body thrown through three sets of walls while the aura was like the sun, covering everything in blinding pastels that seeped from my hands.

My feet hit the floor, and I inhaled slowly, the lights sucking into a single spot that I could only identify as my necklace before I stammered, collapsed, and finally greeted darkness.

If I died now, I'd be okay with it, at least happy to know I took Jull down with me.

EPILOGUE

I turned over in a cloud of a bed, feeling warmth covering my body from head to toe. I inhaled the fresh air. It reminded me of Isla's natural honey scent looming over the breeze. My eyes fluttered open to see if I had died or if I had failed and Jull was alive after all.

Decimus was sitting on the bed, his bare arms carved in bruises and cuts that I didn't recall him having before. He stroked my face with his worn knuckles, his smile tipping when he touched the necklace that rested on my neck.

Yawning lightly, I saw the simple room around us. It was not just a cabin in the middle of Wyoming, but a stunning chamber with marble and gold accents. I could tell we were still in Isla, but I clung to the blanket and sat up, too stiff to do so without a little help.

"Easy," Decimus groaned. "You were out for a while, Ice Princess."

I looked to the sun shining through the open windows, the wind weaving through the bedroom and taunting me with nostalgic memories.

"Did I kill him?"

Decimus nodded without a hint of a frown as he replied, "You did more than that. He was obliterated by that power, Ophelia. I've never seen anything like it."

I held onto my moonstone carefully, trying not to smile. "I think my mother had something to do with that."

He ushered me out of bed, and I tried to follow, clinging to his arm while I took a few steps. I was like a baby deer learning to walk, my legs thin but unblemished by bruises. I didn't even feel a scratch on my body after that fight.

Maybe the light healed me while causing the opposite for Jull.

Decimus pushed the door open, leading me through the long hallway without hinting where we were going. I kept up with his pace, limping as the numbness tainted my limbs. I felt like I'd been asleep for years, but I knew that was impossible.

"Right through here."

He pushed open the door to a large conference room, my heart was relieved as the familiar faces came into view. Terron, Sig, Matteo, Caspian and Elson all leaped from their chairs and rushed over to us. Decimus kept me upright while I was hugged repeatedly by the people I cared about the most.

I wept after seeing that they were all alive and unharmed.

A ping of shock raced through me while I took in the simple joy of our success. "This is crazy," I whispered. "Everyone's alive and—and okay."

"Thanks to you, Ophelia," Terron sighed.

I clung to my necklace more, knowing that my parents were the true heroes here, not me. Everything that had ever happened in my life had led to this moment.

When the advisors all ushered me to the window nearby, the streets filled with people waiting for a signal of hope. They saw me and cheered my name. Confetti fired into the air, and people screamed and hollered in joy. I wept to myself out of happiness to see everyone still alive. And to know that they had faith and hope in me.

I had never been one to receive accolades like this, but lifting my head, I let the euphoria wash over me. In my heart and mind, I accepted my destiny at that moment. I am The Heir Of Isla.

Read on for Book Two In The Realms Of Destiny Series.

KINGPIN
OF
TOPREE

THE REALMS OF DESTINY SERIES

LYSSA LUND

SILVER & GOLD

$\mathcal{T}$opree is a vicious place meant for the dangerous and cunning. As a young woman barely in my twenties, I never thought I would be subjected to this life-style. My cape is tattered on the hem from being in too many scuffles, running so fast through the markets, and getting caught on the exposed tin of the structures that make up my battleground of a home.

This place isn't for the faint of heart, but that's why I love it.

"Run," Elise breathes, giving me a careful look.

I eye her back just as warily, wondering what the trouble is now. She sets down my empty cup of tea, the white porce-lain chipped and redone too many times, but dishes are a delicacy here. The gold chips in my pocket weigh heavily in my loose pants, held onto my frail, boney hips by a belt.

I was really looking forward to something warm to drink, but the hard edge to Elise's hazel eyes warned me to go, signaling that my job for the day was far from over.

I inch my chair back, eyeing the front door to the tea shop. Elise motions to the back door before folding her hands in front of her and returning to a table of brute soldiers and guards, somehow leaking from the wealthy half of Topree and slumming it with us.

The vague sense of familiarity isn't lost on me.

Feeling the weight of the stolen gold in my pocket, I recognize their hateful looks instantly. Not twenty minutes before stumbling into the tea shop, breathless with a mouth full of grit, I was reaching my hands into the pockets of those four men.

It was easy, *too* easy.

"I owe you," I say, tipping my head to Elise while I push my empty teacup aside. "It was delicious."

It's a lie. She must have overheard those men speculating on capturing me or following me back to my boss, but I've been made too quickly even to enjoy something to sip on. The grit has formed a thin layer of mud over my tongue, and I am so dehydrated now that I feel like I'm chewing on sand.

It wouldn't be my worst meal these days, but it doesn't mean I need to take a beating by these soldiers just for them to snatch their gold back. If I get caught, I'm as good as dead or sold in auction to the one percent of wealth in Topree. They don't treat their staff very nicely, but they have hundreds and thousands of peasants to choose from in the slums.

With my smart mouth and daring personality, I know I wouldn't last long waiting on the rich in their ivory towers and glass castles. I'd come in like a raging crocodile, wrapped in ropes and thrashing side to side until I've knocked into everything breakable, blood and chaos dripping from my wounds.

I bleed for trouble but trouble with these four soldiers doesn't suit me right now.

Slipping out the back door, I take off down the dirt roads, my brunette braids bouncing against both of my shoulders while I sprint as fast as I can, my cape whipping at the air behind me. There's a grunting noise behind me. As I flee, my boots stomp against the dirt, an overwhelming sense of urgency filling my empty, starving stomach.

"Stop that girl!" one of them shouts, sprinting after me with their arm extended. I can feel his nails scratching at my cape, ready to yank me back by the loop tied around the hollow of my throat. "Someone stop her!"

No one stops me.

The loyalty these rich blowhards think they will find in the slums is laughable.

"Bounty of a hundred gold pieces!" he hollers next.

Oh crap, I think. *That might do it.*

Someone blindsides me, throwing me into a dead-ended alleyway with the market's tin walls trapping me inside the narrow space. I force myself to sit up, a ringing screaming through my ears while I swallow the fresh clump of dirt that has entered my esophagus.

The body that tackled me to the ground moves back, the soldiers patting him on the shoulder and tossing him a little velvet bag or two of gold coins. I can guarantee I don't have that much in my pockets, but they search me anyways, picking every last gold piece from my clothes until I'm a pound lighter in weight and throbbing in regret.

"Stupid girl," the man up front growls. "Who do you think you are? Stealing from Topree guards. We are peacekeepers."

"Only for those who can pay," I spit, my tone unwelcoming to their baseless scold. "You kill the poor and serve the rich. You have no morality here."

One of them chuckles, counting the gold and redistributing it to the other three. "You did good work, pickpocket. Almost eighty gold pieces. You must do this professionally."

"I do what I have to."

"You do as you're told," he growls, pulling a long knife

from the sheath on his belt. He pulls the blade's edge against my shirt, cutting the hem of my neckline and exposing the black ink tattooed on the ridge of my collarbone. "Four-hundred-and-twenty-two."

I swallow at the three numbers forever poked into my pale, lightly freckled skin. I didn't want the tattoo, but I was held down and given the brand anyway. It's nothing more than a sign of property—he was right, too. I am a pickpocketing thief full-time, and the number on my shoulder exposes that to their beady eyes.

"You've got to be kidding me," he snarls, pushing his knife back into its hip holder. "You work for Renner, don't you?"

I nod somberly. "Yes, I do."

"How did you know that?" one of the other soldiers asks, his uniform a tight black outfit with red seams.

The man with the knife rocks back on his heels, staring at me while I cower in the dirt at his unpolished boots. "The number. Four-two-two. It's a sector identifier. She's a bandit for her section of Topree. Four is the regiment number. She works and probably lives in section four. Two is the middle number. There are three levels of thieves. One is livelihood goods like food and merchandise. Two is money. Three is life."

"Like assassins?" one of them ponders.

The wiser of the soldiers nodded. "Yeah, but not this one. She's a money thief. Nothing more."

"So, what's the last number mean? It's another two."

"Age," I blurt.

The soldier smiles wickedly. "It's the age she was when she was *recruited*."

I swallow at the dirty looks they give me, judging me like I signed up for this life. I can't help that I was born in section four, one of the most dangerous edges of Topree, where the marsh and desert meet. I was a toddler, sold into the thievery trade. It's not like my life was set up for much else. At least my mother got some money in exchange for throwing me to the kingpin wolves.

"Well, what do you want to do with her?"

"We could take her to Francis. He needs another maid in his office."

"She's not cut out for that," the knowing soldier replies with a modest shrug. He plucks a hand into his pocket and flicks a silver coin toward me, the pathetic money hitting the dust between my hands. "There you go, girl. Scurry back to your boss."

"Without punishment? She stole from Topree soldiers."

"Trust me," he taunts. "Going back to Renner with nothing but a little silver chip is punishment enough. She will suffer more out here in the markets and running the streets. Leave her be. We have work to do."

I swallow while they turn, eyeing the silver coin. I spot the velvet bag left on the soldier's hip, bouncing with the weight of gold and wealth that I could only dream of acquiring. While not my best idea, I can't help but push my luck off the cliff.

Scurrying up to my feet, I latch onto the soldier's hips and hurl myself in front of him, hanging onto his sides with false tears in my eyes. If not so dehydrated, I could push more tears from my gritty, irritated eyelids.

"Please, sir," I beg, hiccuping through my cracked lips while the other soldiers snicker at my pathetic plea. "I need money to give to my boss. I have a family to provide for. I haven't eaten in three days—I couldn't even enjoy my tea before you came after me. Please, sir."

He caresses my cheek and nods, his grin becoming a salacious curl. "Poor thing. Little street rat is hungry."

"Starving," I choke, my hand brushing the velvet bag on

his hip and finding the twine cord that keeps it to his belt. "I just need one gold piece to bring back. Please, sir."

He toys with my braid and looks over me carefully. I can see the gears working in his head, but when he looks at the others, they give him a firm shake of their heads. Their disapproval is enough for him to wind his hand back and strike his knuckles against my warm, filthy cheek.

I'm ripped sideways from his body, thrown into the dirt once more before he steps over me, and they leave like a pack of cackling hyenas. Blood seeps from my nostrils, but I brush it away with the back of my hand, trembling slightly while I steady myself upright again.

A passerby darts into the alleyway, kneeling before me.

I tuck the stolen velvet bag into my cape and get lost in his emerald eyes.

"Are you okay, miss? I saw those men attack you," he grumbles, his stunning features like something from a statue in the upscale part of Topree. He had a chiseled jaw, vibrant eyes, and full lips set in a handsome smirk. "Here, take this." He hands me a handkerchief, and I press it to my pulsing upper lip. "Why did they attack you like that?"

"Because they are wealthy, and they can," I mutter, knowing this man in a button-down shirt and clean jeans isn't from around Topree. Maybe Earth, but considering his flawless features, I assume he's an Isla resident. "Who are you?"

"Sig Hughes. And you?"

"Rue Padron," I reply, dapping away the blood on my lips. "I don't need any help, sir. I am fine now. I should just get going before they come back."

I stand nearly a foot shorter than the well-dressed stranger. I offer him his handkerchief back, but it's doused in my blood. He waves for me to keep it, so I do, tucking it into my pocket where the velvet bag of coins rests.

When I push past him, he stops me, extending his palm to reveal a handful of gold and silver coins. "Here, take this," he urges.

I freeze, unsure if this is a trap. No one just *gives* out money in Topree. You either are rich enough to surround yourself with it like a greedy cow, or you're too poor to do anything other than steal it. Still, he pushes his hand out further for me to take the coins, and I do.

"Th—Thanks," I mutter, wondering what the catch is.

He smiles soberly, something sad in his handsome features making my stomach turn. "You're welcome, Rue. If you ever need anything, I have a house in section two. It's the only green house on the street. Come by if you run into more trouble. I have some pull with Topree soldiers."

"Because you're an immigrant?"

He cocks his head sideways. "What?"

"You're from Isla, right?"

He folds his arms over his broad chest, eyeing me cautiously. "Yeah. How did you know that?"

"You're too striking to be from here," I admit. "And clean. *Way* too clean. Plus, no one just hands out gold pieces. You have to work yourself to the bone out here just for some silver specks, and even then, you'll get robbed before you make it home at night."

"Robbed by a woman like you?"

I hiss at his stoic tone, and he notices my recoil.

"I didn't mean to insult you, Rue," he says. "But I saw the velvet bag in your pocket. It looks a lot like the one that soldier was carrying moments ago."

"I have a family," I bite again, the oldest sympathy card in the book. While not a total lie, it's certainly not the whole truth. "I have to do something."

"Go," he sighs, nodding me forward. "Take my money to

your boss. Keep what you took from the soldiers for yourself. If you need anything again, come find me."

I leave on that note, worried he's trailing me to the outskirts of section three. There has to be a catch with his generosity, but I can't stick around and find out. Instead, I hurry back to section four. The sun is starting to dip down out of the sky, and the soldiers who protect the rich will be at the pubs in the most dangerous corners of my section at night.

Walking alone in the dark out here isn't the wisest move —especially when the entitled come out to play with the poor.

I skip to the warehouse near the marsh, my feet kicking through the dust while I approach the tin door. A rusted portion of the wall gives me a glimpse into the warehouse, the lights off unusually early for Renner, who primarily works at night. Still, I knock and let myself in, coming into a cold room with an eerie aura.

Flicking the light on, my heart falls into my stomach.

Renner is on the floor, covered in blood. He is motionless in death.

WILD

I inch back a step, bumping into a brute of muscle that lingers behind me now. I wince, jumping forward only to see more men like him emerging from the shadows. Being careful not to step on my lifeless boss, I back myself into a corner and hold my breath, looking desperately for a way out of this predicament.

"Easy, guys," a slithering voice hums from afar. A lean, toweringly tall man stalks forward from the next room, holding a long cane with a gold figurine on top that looks like a dragon's head, breathing golden fire from its snout. "Who might you be?"

"Rue," I say, trying to sound confident, but the smell of iron blood taints my senses. "Who—who are you?"

"I'm the new owner of section four," he sighs, flicking his wrist. The large men all back away submissively, leaving this guy, who is as tall and thin as a sugarcane sprout, to tower over me. "I guess that means I'm your new boss, girl. Come into my office. We can talk."

I follow him, careful not to look into Renner's wide, open eyes. Flies crawl over his dead body while I hurry away from the repulsive scene, fearing the worst for my fate. The tall man leads me into Renner's old office, somewhere that I never liked being while he was alive. He was a filthy old man with terrible manners and a temper only a crook would adore.

He beat me for falling short on gold pieces and threatened my sister's life. She's the only one I have left, and I won't let her fall victim again. I must protect her at all costs, even if it means bartering, begging, and stealing my way through life.

"Take a seat," he sighs, circling the long, mahogany desk. He kicks his jacket back and sits down like he's some kind of royalty, the black of his eyes second to that of his greasy hair. He pushes a tea kettle forward and a cup not riddled with cracks. "Tell me about what you did for Renner, girl."

I pour myself some, still salivating for the tea I was deprived of earlier by the sudden ambush. Still, I fold my legs into the chair and take a long sip of the warm drink.

"I'm a thief," I mutter into my cup.

He nods knowingly, motioning to my shirt. "Show me the numbers."

Clutching my cup in one hand, I yank my shirt collar sideways so he can see the tattoo faded against my pale frame. His smile grows, and he signals for me to release it, so I do and focus on the tea instead. He taps his fingers along the ridge of his desk.

"Section four, loyal," he hums. "A money thief. You've been at this a long time, Rue. Who sold you into the trade?"

"How do you know I was sold?" I ponder.

"I doubt toddlers are jumping to be thieves when they grow up."

"You're not from here, are you? That's all there is in section four. You can get a job in section three at the markets. Section two has some rich folk living in the slums—

they pay well for menial things. Section one, the wealthy, they go through maids like they do t-shirts."

"Then there's you," he sighs. "A little young thing in section four. You've got a bruise forming on your cheek and you're filthy. Do you own a shower, Rue? Do you have running water?"

"I go to the sulfur shallows," I admit, a natural sulfur spring that burns with heat and steam and has a nasty stench, but it cleans me as well as any shower. "The bruise is from a soldier. I ran across a few of them earlier today, but it's okay. I wasn't followed."

"Good girl," he taunts. When he notices I'm out of tea, he nods, allowing me to have more. "So, how much did Renner usually make you turn over daily?"

"At least ten gold pieces."

"That's a lot. More than the others I've come across today. They say he only made them fetch two or three a day. You must be proactive in your work."

"I do what I can," I mutter into the teacup. "I have a younger sister. She's ill. He says if I turn in ten a day, he will provide me her medication."

He perks up with that information. "Really? Tell me about your sister."

"She's not technically my sister. My mother sold me to Renner when I was two years old. When I was thirteen, I found her bundled up on the warehouse steps as a baby. They were going to give her to Renner to be a thief like me, but I intercepted her. He said I could keep her as mine if I did more than double the workload."

"You're very charismatic," he sighs. "What is her ailment?"

"She doesn't have an immune system, I think," I say. "She's always getting food poisoning, the flu—all kinds of stuff. Renner gave me a vial of clear liquid one day to help her get better, and it worked, so she has to take it every day now."

He opens the desk, pulls out a little vial of clear fluid, and holds it to the light between us. "Well, that explains all the kelp extract in his desk drawers. This stuff is a rarity here. Only available on Earth."

I swallow hard, watching him toy with the vial that means the world to me—and more.

"You're going to bring me ten gold pieces a day, Rue," he says casually. "Any day you come up short will lead to punishment. Three days in a row of missed payments will result in your life. Your sister won't be harmed, and I won't make her work if you can shift your loyalty from Renner to me."

My blood runs ice cold. "Ye—Yes, sir."

"Good," he hums, rolling the vial across the desk. It falls into my lap, and I relax, watching him fill a small bag full of medication I could never dream of getting my hands on all at once. He scoots it over, but when I reach for it, he pulls it back. "Ah, ah, ah. Where's mine?"

I thumb through ten gold pieces in my pocket and hand them over, watching his eyes light up. He finally gives me the bag of medicine, and I cling to it with my life, feeling anxious to get home and get my sister into better shape.

When I stand to leave, he does the same, and my curiosity overwhelms me. Clinging to the bag of kelp extract, I turn to face his daunting height over me.

"What's your name?"

His smile is crooked and sinister, his teeth brilliantly white, proving what realm he's from. "My name is Cornelius Breech. You can call me Core."

I tip my head at his peculiar name, but it's not the weirdest I've heard today.

"Boss, another one is here with today's bounty," a burly man calls from the warehouse.

Core ushers me out, glancing over my shoulder while

another stunned thief realizes Renner has been killed and overthrown in power. I can feel Core's dark eyes on me as I hurry out of the warehouse with medication, and extra gold pieces, in hand.

I don't wait around to be robbed, sprinting through the forest nearby and pitching myself into the marshy landscape. I jump through the veins and dart around the large, hollowed trees filled with nasty critters, leaping through the disgusting water until I come across the rope dangling from the tallest tree in the swamp.

Climbing to the top, I hold onto the bag with my teeth and anchor my way up into the tree limbs. Our shack is well-built up here, branching into a lofty paradise connected with wood walkways, rope swings for escape, and a view worth dying for.

I step onto the platform and hoist the rope up to the railing to ensure we won't be ambushed at night. The sun sets over Topree, the sand riled by the wind finally settling as the sky burns a stunning orange and pink streaks the dull gray skies. I can see over the packed slums of the sections outside of the rich squadron.

Section one is nothing but ivory towers and glass walls, the homes and pampered world so amazing to witness—even from my makeshift treehouse.

"Rue," a weak voice calls. "Is that—is that you?"

"I'm here," I breathe, pushing the cloth curtain aside to see Mare bent over on her mattress, her face flushed and her lightly tanned skin splotchy with dark and light spots. She's breaking down in every possible way, but she's stronger than to let this sickness kill her anytime soon. "I've got medicine," I add, dropping the bag of vials on her bed. "Lots of it."

"Wow," she breathes, trembling all over like she's cold, but the sweat on both of our scalps proves otherwise. "How did you get so much this time? Renner must be feeling generous."

"Renner's dead," I tell her, a little relieved by that fact. "Some new guy took over. He gave me all of this, I guess to ensure I won't defect section four and that I'll still bring him his bounty like I did for Renner. Speaking of which," I add, emptying the gold from my pockets. "We will need this."

"Oh my," she gasps. "How did you—who did you—what?"

"Soldiers," I say. "I took the coin purse from one of them. The loose change is actually from some guy I ran into today. He's from Isla. He gave me all of that."

She gives me a skeptical look. "Really? He just *handed* you gold and silver coins?"

"I wouldn't lie if I stole from him," I reply. "He *gave* it to me. Even told me where he lives if I need more. He's harmless, sis. I promise."

Still, her apprehension is clear in her brown eyes, and she tucks back her light brunette curls behind her ears. "You've got enough coins to go get some new pants," she says. "You need something that fits you, Rue. Your clothes are dropping off your body."

"Don't worry about me," I insist. "I'm fine. I promise. I'll get us some food tomorrow and maybe another blanket for you. You're shivering at night and your teeth chatter in your sleep. Makes me nervous."

She rolls her eyes. "You sleep on a ball on the wood floor, and you want to get me a blanket? Why won't you spend your money on yourself sometimes? You can't take care of me without taking care of yourself."

"I can, and I will," I breathe, helping her back onto her narrow mattress. "Just relax. I'm going to see about fetching some water from town later when everyone is asleep. I think I can break the coin lock off the spout and get some for free this time."

"You're wild," she whispers, giving up and lying in bed at last.

I push her hair aside and urge her to take a vial of medication. She settles into sleep rather quickly, my heart breaking at her worsening condition. She's innocent and young—she should have a better life than this one. She says I'm wild because I'd do anything to protect her.

I pray she never understands why I have to protect her. She's too delicate for this realm, for these men, and they're domineering ways. Truth be told, Topree is eighty-percent male. Females don't live long out here, and when they do, they end up chew toys for the wealthy and the strong.

Losing Mare would be the worst thing to ever happen in my miserable life.

Wild is nothing. My needs are secondary.

Defense is everything.

PUB GOSSIP

*M*ost people think it's too dangerous to go around Topree at night, so that's when I find it the best to get tasks done. I know I need to get some market food tomorrow, but my stomach is doing turns in my gut. I can't trick my body into thinking I'm full of mud and dirt anymore; I need a meal.

Sending the last pail of water up to the treehouse, I eye the dark swamp. It's cool tonight, the air light without any wind and the humidity low as it hangs over the realm. Glancing up at the treehouse once more, I know I should call it a night and go to bed, but the pull of town draws me in too much to ignore.

I'll be back before midnight, I promise myself, as I sneak back out into the desert of section four. Lingering outside the pub in section three, the smell of barbeque and freshly pulled pork tempts my senses. I drool in anticipation, slipping into the rowdy bar.

I pause, seeing that I'm the only female inside the packed joint. It's not uncommon, but it's unnerving all the same. Finding a seat in the corner, I push my back into the wall and down the glass of murky well water the waiter slides before me.

Sinking into my seat, I take a long, deep drag of cigarette-tainted air and exhale.

The waiter clears his throat obnoxiously. "Miss, will you be able to pay for a meal?"

I reached into my pocket and let him see a small stash of gold and silver, just in case I couldn't break the lock off the town waterspout. When he's convinced I won't rip off the pub, he takes my order and only visits to refill my cup of water now and again.

I eye the crowd in the meantime, feeling them size me up carefully for several reasons. Some might try to take me home tonight, some might offer to buy my time and anything else I could offer them, and others might just work for the one percent, meaning they will drug my water and haul me off to Sector One to be a maid.

As long as I have the tattoo on my collarbone, I'm safe. It ensures my livelihood is already owned unless my boss, now Mr. Core, feels like sending me away. That's when the tattoo is cut from my flesh, and the ties to section four are ripped away from me forever.

I wouldn't miss this world, but I would kill to return to Mare.

"You hear about Cornelius? He slit Renner's throat and took over the section," one man says nearby.

His buddy replies with a blasé shrug of his broad shoulders. "It won't last. Renner was a hard-ass, and no one dared face him. Now that he's out of the way, everyone will try to have this new guy slaughtered."

"All about control," the man harrumphs. "It's pathetic, too. He came from section one and thinks he can just swoop in and play bandit-keeper. Yeah, right. He's going to lose control of those filthy street rats in no time."

I wince at the slur to me and my kind. I didn't dream of being a thief as a toddler, I just dreamed of freedom from Renner. I've never known any other life than this one.

"Hey, girl," one of them grunts.

I look through the mess of my bangs that sit loosely against my forehead. "Yes, sir?"

They both exchange a look before moving to my table, clutching pints of beer.

"You worked for Renner, didn't you?"

Before I can reply or shoo them away, the one beside me pulls my shirt sideways, exposing my tattoo. I look away, and they both chuckle to themselves.

"So, you've met the new guy, huh?"

Swallowing hard, I nod. "Yeah, I have. Core."

"Awe, she's on a first-name basis with her new boss," he chortles. "Very cute."

"She's not so bad herself," the other hums, giving me a narrow look.

I push further into the corner, the waiter dropping my food off but doing little to address the bullies at my table. He doesn't get paid enough to start fights with the drunks in here. I pull my plate to the side, my wrist caught in one of their hands. He yanks me right back to the spot beside him, his breath tainted with tobacco and liquor.

"How much would that new boss of yours take to cut you loose?"

"Too much for you to afford," a gravelly voice says from nearby. My eyes draw up Cornelius' thin frame. "Let go of my property. Now."

The two men don't hesitate, proving how intimidated they are by Core and his bodyguards. He slides into the seat beside me, flicking his wrist toward the waiter. He orders a beer, pushes my food in front of me, and his posse sits across from us and at other tables because there are not enough chairs.

The pub carries on as usual like nothing ever happened.

"You draw too much attention," he points out, speaking under his breath. "You should work on that, girl. Keep your head down. Don't talk to strangers."

"They came over to me," I reply, carefully picking at my food. "I don't look for trouble."

"Rich, coming from the thief."

"You're the leader of the thieves," I snarl on impulse. "Doesn't make you any better."

He leans sideways, speaking into my ear. "I could kill you and not even blink an eye at your death, Rue. I could sell you to the lowest bidder in Sector One and pay them to make your life miserable. The difference between you and me is clear. You have no power. I have it all."

I wince at his words, but he smiles and returns to nursing his beer.

"I have a task for you tonight."

I sit up straighter, picking at my food. "What is it?"

"I need you to create a diversion. I have business to tend to on the marsh river. There's a small canal that runs through Sector Two. It has a militant guard on post at night. I need them to pull back so I can load up some cargo into my boat and sail away."

I eye the rest of the brutes that Core keeps with him like a security blanket. "What kind of diversion?"

"You told me earlier today that you had a run-in with some soldiers," he breathes, stroking my cheek. "I think you should use your head and devise a plan, sweetheart. Okay?"

"They'll kill me," I admit with a heavy sigh. "I stole from them twice today. If they spot me again, they'll sell me to Sector One."

"No, because you won't be caught," he points out. "Just do

your job. Do as I say. Otherwise, I think you'll be more afraid of my punishment than the soldiers' plans for you."

Looking sideways, I can only nod, knowing I don't have a choice. I'm not sure what business Core has with the canal or Sector Two, but I can't deny him a request. He owns my life, and the tattoo that keeps me prisoner in this world is the only thing saving me from something worse.

I may hate the demons I have, but at least they're demons I *know*.

"When do you need this done?"

"Soon," he says, playing with the rim of his glass. "I just need you to do everything right, get my shipment sent off tonight, and I'll get you as much medication as possible for your sister."

My body groans with hope. "Okay. I'll be there."

"Good," he sighs, taking one final gulp and tossing the waiter enough gold to cover both of our charges. "I knew I liked you, Rue. You're proving to be a very handy ally."

I don't mention his not-so-subtle threats if I don't partici-pate, so I'm not sure why he thinks I'm doing this willingly. I have to abide by his rule. He's the new boss. I finish my meal, and the waiter settles the payment for whatever Core gave him.

Pulling the hood of my cape back up, I sprint through town, heading for Sector Two, where I know the canal lies. I keep pace until I'm at the edge of Sector Three, slowing down and scoping the place out. The homes are slightly taller and not so cramped in size and space between them. I find the highest house on the outskirts of town and scale the tin wall with ease.

Pulling myself to the roof, I lie flat on my stomach and let the moonlight cascade down my back. I inch forward, spying the militants near the canal, none looking familiar from my earlier altercation.

"Okay, Rue," I mutter, counting each one and then searching for weapons strapped to their hips. "You got this. You can do this. Just be fast, don't get caught. Be fast, don't get—"

"Hey! Get down from there! It's a spy!"

I swallow, seeing a soldier stumble out of a house nearby, his eyes locked on my position on top of the house. There's no other choice now. I have to run. The other soldiers follow, screaming for me to stop and come down, but I leap roof to roof until I'm well into Sector Two.

There are no boundaries between sections except for section one, the tall, guarded walls between zones coming closer while I sprint from the soldiers below.

I jump between houses, missing the roof by inches and slicing my side on a tin metal gable. I hit the dirt hard, already splattered in blood, while the soldiers catch up to me, circling me with guns drawn.

They're not the same soldiers from the incident earlier today, which makes me wonder why they chased after me. Laying on the roof of a house is hardly a crime out here, and even if they just saw me stab a man in the street, they wouldn't arrest me.

One of them pulls my shirt sideways, reading the numbers printed on my skin.

"She's a Cornelius rat," he barks.

"I'm not a rat," I reply.

"She's a dead woman," one of them grumbles. "Send a message to your new boss that his little rats aren't welcome outside of Sector Four." He steadies the pistol towards my head and pauses. "Your kind should just be eradicated from Topree for good."

I hold my breath while I wait to be killed, fearing that Mare will never heal from her sickness. She will die alone in the trees, unable to care for herself in such a condition. It will be my fault, too.

Before the gun is fired, a familiar voice calls from around the corner. "Wait, she's with me."

The soldiers stop, and we all turn to see a familiar man with light hair and eyes like emeralds.

"And who are you?"

"I'm an advisor from Isla. Rue Padron is my responsibility. She cannot be harmed, or Topree will be breaking treaty with the advisors' board of Isla."

My voice catches in my throat, unable to utter a word while the soldiers give up rather quickly. I knew Sig was from Isla, I could tell from his stunning features. But to know he's an advisor is something else. He's like a prince in his realm, and now I owed him my life.

Continue reading Rue and Sig's story here!

ACKNOWLEDGMENTS

THANK YOU, THANK YOU, THANK YOU to all who have supported me while I worked on this story. Especially my ARC readers, for your thoughts and critiques.

My parents, for always believing I can do anything I set my mind on. Over the years, you have done so much to lift me up and help me grow. I love you both so much. There will never be enough words to tell you how much.

To my daughters Maria and Amanda - You both are and always will be my sunshine.

My sisters, Steff and Becca, for reading my stories first, leaving 5 stars reviews, lol, and being so supportive. I love you - I love the rest of my siblings too, just as much. :)

Alice - for the honest feedback and proofreading. You are amazing and so generous with your time. Thank you.

To my advance release copy readers. Thank you for your support and encouragement and for catching those last straggling typos. It really helps to see things through, knowing you are waiting in the wings to read!

Maureen from www.WORDTINKERER.com

Thank you for your help with polishing up the finished product! It made all the difference.

And Craigypoo - for everything.

ALSO BY LYSSA LUND

Shadows Of Dark And Light

A Touch Of Prophesy

The Dark King's Heart

The Sylvan Wilds

The Borderland Guardians

The Blizzard Crossing

Beyond Aorel

Realms Of Destiny Series

The Lost Heir Of Isla

Kingpin Of Topree

Maya Rodgers Mysteries

Deadly Dynasty

Ink and Blood

Brushed By Danger - Coming Soon

Lake Minnetonka Cozy Mysteries

Secrets Buried

Petals Of Peril

ABOUT LYSSA LUND

About Lyssa Lund

Lyssa Lund discovered her love of reading in first grade when she discovered Hans Christian Anderson and The Brothers Grimm fairy tales.

Lyssa is an avid reader and writer who understands wanting to escape and be carried away by the story. Lyssa aims for the best in strong female characters, heart-of-gold alpha heroes, mystery, suspense, and heartwarming romance while keeping it clean.

Freebies

Do you like FREEBIE books?
Sign up for my newsletter and get book recommendations
and special offers for my readers to get books for free!

Get notified about early-releases by registering here.

You can also visit my website www.lyssalund.com

Join my Facebook Group Here: https://www.facebook.com/
lyssaLund/

AFTERWORD

Thank you for reading my books. I know you have many choices, and I sincerely appreciate you choosing mine.

As an indie author, it can be hard to get the word out about my books, and the most important tool I have is word of mouth from readers like you.

If you enjoyed my book, it would be very helpful if you could leave a review to encourage other readers to take a chance on my work.

I am on Goodreads, Bookbub, and Amazon.

I also love private feedback. You can reach me at hello@ lyssalund.com

xoxo, Lyssa

Kingpin Of Topree

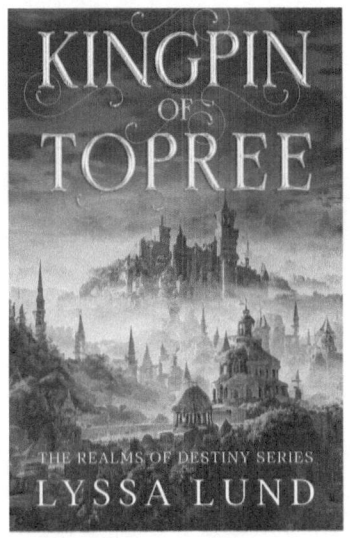